DEATH AT THE ALTAR

Mary Shelley Investigations
Book Three

Donna Gowland

SAPERE
BOOKS

DEATH AT THE ALTAR

Published by Sapere Books.

24 Trafalgar Road, Ilkley, LS29 8HH

saperebooks.com

ISBN:

To my father John Anthony Taylor
"If you can imagine it, you can achieve it..."

CHAPTER ONE

London, 1815

Mary Wollstonecraft Godwin kept the ghosts with her. No matter where she went, she was never free from them and now the vision of her baby daughter — so pale, so tiny, so cold — was the most vivid of all, pushing even the ghost of her mother aside. Mary glanced at Percy Shelley, his delicate porcelain features cast with a fresh heaviness that ridged at the sides of his mouth, like the folded sails of a paper boat. They walked to the carriage in silence, hands held lightly like promises, the weight of their grief pushing them apart.

Salt Hill had been as charming and verdant as ever; their sojourn should have been the perfect tonic. If anywhere could stop the ghosts, it was there, but Mary didn't need a mirror to know that her grief was as deeply carved into her features as Percy's. It was there in the deep shadows under her eyes from the broken nights, which brought her daughter to her in vivid nightmares and then snatched her away afresh each morning. Mary hadn't seen a sunrise this year; she was sure there had been one, she just hadn't noticed. She had become a shell of her former self and took no notice in the beauty of the world around her.

Mary accepted Percy's hand up into the carriage. She knew that he looked at her with pity rather than desire. He had done his best to conceal it, but it had been clear when she'd slipped off her undergarments, exposing the newly prominent ribs and bird-like frame, shrivelled by grief. Percy coughed and smiled at her, but it was too late to conceal his true feelings. So much passed unsaid between them these days. Their previous intimacy had evaporated like a fog. She saw that every time he looked at her. Mary understood, because it was the same for her. They would get over the physical distance — it wasn't as if they hadn't done so before — but this unfamiliar terrain, this wordless gulf between them that swallowed their pain and regurgitated it with a strange, shallow politeness, was what truly haunted her.

The countryside woke up around them as the carriage made its way back to the city, the slow spring day stretching into life, lifting the early morning grey. Mary willed herself to feel something, but her grief was as immovable as the hills outside the carriage window. Black smoke belched into the sky from the city beyond them. Caught in the wind, some smoke drifted in through the window and stung her eyes. They sprung quickly to tears, her grief a constant companion waiting for the opportunity to speak. For a moment she was thrust back into the nightmare that had plagued her nights: she was walking along the passageway towards her daughter's cradle, and for a brief, delicious moment, the baby — Clara — was alive and all Mary's love and hope swelled afresh. She would never forget Clara's face, the fragility of her tiny hands, the spidery eyelashes, the cupid's bow lips she'd inherited from her father. Approaching the baby, she mistook death for serenity, and reached out a hand, expecting to feel the gentle heartbeat beneath. There was none. Each time her mind replayed that fateful evening, Mary prayed for a different result.

She hadn't realised she'd been sobbing until she felt the warmth of Percy's hand against hers. They had been intimate together on their holiday, but it was mechanical and soulless, with none of their earlier tenderness. She felt like a ghost, walking through the echo chambers of her life as if it were nothing more than a museum. Mary looked at Percy's hand and thought of the child's hand she would never hold, she bit her lip to stop the tears from falling again.

Eventually, the carriage drew up outside their new residence in Bishopsgate, and the gentle burbling of the nearby stream made her soul sigh with a welcome approximation of peace. But it was accompanied, as it always was, with a gnawing sensation in her stomach as she looked beyond the trees to the house's windows and thought of her sister, Claire, contained within it. Perhaps Claire had finally moved out of their house, giving them space to grieve their loss in peace.

'Well, Mary, we are home.' Percy put an arm around her. 'It will be different now. It will be better. Claire will be kinder.'

Mary gathered her bag. Poor Percy, always wanting to see the best in people. She did not harbour such childish illusions.

'Claire does not have the vocabulary for kindness.'

'You may be underestimating her.'

'I doubt it.' Mary pursed her lips, ignoring the coldness that swelled up inside her.

'Perhaps she has gone out for a stroll. Come on.' Percy jumped down from the carriage. Mary hesitated. She knew that hoping Claire had left the house was wishful thinking. Claire only took herself out if she was following Percy like a faithful lapdog. Claire was always waiting in the wings, an enthusiastic understudy. Mary nodded, accepted Percy's help from the carriage, and brushed down her dress to disguise her shaking hands. When she had composed herself, she looked up and took a deep breath, ignoring the nausea creeping up her throat at the thought of going back into the house. If she was going to keep mind and soul together, she would need every ounce of strength she had.

'That's odd.' Percy frowned as they reached the open front door. 'Where are the staff?' He turned towards Mary as if she'd have the answers. They had only recently hired them. A small sum of money from Percy's grandfather had elevated their standard of living.

'Have we returned on their day off?' Mary replied.

'No,' Percy shook his head and pushed the door open. He had an innate ability to pinpoint the exact movements of staff and spot any deviation from their schedule with alarming accuracy, that Mary thought could only be an innate talent of his breeding. Together they crept through the house, Percy moving cautiously ahead as if expecting to find a burglar at work.

'What the blazes!'

Percy stormed into the study. Papers were scattered everywhere, his beloved Greek statues thrown around and left decapitated, armless and limbless on the floor, his expensive books torn from their covers, his quills shorn of every feather.

'Someone has been in here!' he yelled, rushing out of the room. 'Claire, Claire!'

Panic washed over Mary. If they were still here, they may have gone to the baby's room. She sped up the stairs, aware of Percy's heavy footsteps immediately behind hers. She turned into the nursery and the sight of the devastation made her sink to the ground.

'Who would do such a thing?' All the furniture was upturned and broken, the baby's drawers all turned out and empty.

'No, no, no!' she wailed, scrambling to pick up the shards of broken wood, desperate to claw back anything that had once held her baby. 'Who would do this? Who?'

'Claire,' Percy hissed, turning on his heels and racing back down the stairs.

Mary followed, her own anger tempered by the fear of what Percy was about to do. She grabbed his arm. 'Percy, please, do not make the situation worse.'

She could smell smoke again. The closer they got to the garden, the stronger it became. Mesmerised, they walked towards it and Mary gasped at what she saw — a huge fire burning every last memory of Clara, every parchment of Shelley's poetry, everything that they valued.

'What are you doing?' Mary lunged at Claire, who was standing by the fire with a wild, indignant look on her face. Percy held her back, their roles momentarily reversed. His arms tightened their hold as she struggled within them. If Claire wanted a battle, Mary was more than happy to give her one.

'We need to put it out.' Percy pointed a finger toward the growing flames.

Seeing that he was right, and that if they didn't put it out soon everything would be destroyed, Mary tempered the temptation to throw Claire onto the bonfire and with a supernatural calm, slowly walked towards her.

'I see you are having a clear-out, how considerate of you to get things ready for our return,' Mary said, swallowing down the bile that rose in her throat. 'Perhaps it is time to put out the fire, Claire?'

Claire nodded silently and together the sisters walked over to the stream adjacent to the garden, where each filled buckets with water, sloshing a path back to the flames. The fire, like Claire's anger, was quickly extinguished.

Percy's latest manuscript lay in the ashes of the fire. It was singed but legible. He grabbed at it, forgetting that moments earlier it had been aflame. He jigged the paper between his fingers before dropping it again. Claire and Mary laughed, a moment of shared feeling among the rubble of their lives. Mary always copied his poetry into her own journal, so there was no reason for him to make such a show of their retrieval.

'There you go.' Mary handed Percy the poem. He clutched it to his chest with a father's tenderness that made Mary's heart ache. Now that her baby had gone, there was nothing so precious to her, no relief from the torment of loss, and certainly no replacement. In that moment, she envied Percy his words, his ability to express his inner feelings, even when emotions were easy to find but hard to articulate. Claire had destroyed the baby's possessions. There would be no more cuddling the baby's blanket, willing herself to remember how it felt to hold her; no more gentle placing of the cap on the baby's head or manoeuvring her tiny arms into pretty chambray dresses. The demolition of that experience left Mary with a hollow feeling that felt somehow liberating. She felt weightless as a bird. Now, there was nothing.

'I think I will draw a bath,' Claire whispered. Mary turned to look at her. Claire's hands were covered in soot, her gown ruined. Mary was well accustomed to simultaneously hating and loving her sister, but whatever tolerance she had for her sister had gone up in flames.

'A capital idea,' Percy replied. Mary raised her eyebrows; how easily his anger had been extinguished. How easily they had fallen back into their old ways; how sensitive they were to Claire's feelings — putting them ahead of their own.

Claire nodded and bowed her head as she walked past them back into the house. Mary and Percy stood together, watching the remnants of their former life cooling into ash. Percy shuffled his feet.

'I'm sorry, Mary, this is all my fault. You said she should leave months ago. I never thought she was capable of something like this…' His words faltered and were replaced by tears.

Mary put her arms around Percy. He collapsed into them and she held him up, as she always did. This was the honesty she'd been waiting for, an acknowledgement of their grief, a sharing in it. They had gone away to bring them back together, but had needed to come back home to be reminded of their bond.

'I think,' Mary said, 'it's about time Claire moved out.'

'How curious that we should both receive mail on the same day.' Claire eyed Mary with a narrow gaze. Mary ignored the comment and turned her attention to opening her own envelope. Claire rounded her shoulders, hunching over the letter until safely out of the room. Percy, lying on the settle, yawned laconically before speaking.

'Who is your letter from?'

'It is not a letter, it is an invitation to a wedding,' replied Mary. She had grown so accustomed to their ostracization from London's polite society that the thought of returning to it, however briefly, made her stomach turn.

'A wedding?' Percy clapped his hands together. 'How capital! Whose wedding is it?'

'Adele Somerton, a neighbour of the Barretts in Dundee.'

'The Barretts?' Percy frowned. 'Do I know anything about them?'

'My father experienced a fancy that I should have some schooling in Scotland? He said it would "broaden my horizons and improve my health", but I think it was nothing more than a ruse to get me away from my step-mother.' Mary shuddered, the memory of her father's relationship with Mary Jane springing back into her mind. She remembered every furrowed brow, every acerbic word, every small but significant cruelty.

Escaping to Dundee had been a great escape, a temporary but life-changing reprieve.

'Ah, yes, the Barretts.' Percy sighed. 'Have you heard from Lilian lately?'

Mary folded her arms. Percy knew this was a touchy subject. Lilian was one of the first people she'd told of her relationship with Percy, and Lilian's disapproval of it ranked highest, especially when considered against the questionable match she had made for herself.

'No, and I do not imagine I will, so long as she stays with *him*.' She shivered, unable to even bring herself to utter the name of Lilian's husband. If romance novels had taught her it was possible to love at first sight, then Reginald Ullmann had taught her it was also possible to hate someone too. How he'd destroyed Lilian's personality, pulling away at her confidence as if pulling off petals. His wife's sister, his mission Lilian's seduction. How deplorable a man he was, how scheming. Lilian's heart had been swept away by him at a time when her family was so deeply entrenched in grief they had no mind towards caution. He had been wooing Lilian whilst his wife was dying and all Mary could do about it was send written warnings and plead with Lilian to be careful. Contemptible man. A shot of panic raced through her. He wouldn't be there, would he? The Somertons had lived in the house next to The Cottage on Ferry Road, but it was likely that Adele had found herself removed from Lilian's life by Reginald's controlling behaviour; something Mary had experienced for herself when she had visited them.

'Who is Adele to marry?'

'It doesn't say.' Mary held out the invitation for Percy's inspection. It was brief, written on the plainest of parchment with the scantest of details. No groom's name was given, only the time, date and location of the wedding.

'Next week!' Percy cried. 'It does not give us much time to arrange transport to Doddingley.'

'I've never even heard of the place.' Mary shrugged. 'Anyway, an invitation given with so little preparation time is nothing more than a polite gesture. There was never an expectation of acceptance.'

'Nonsense.' Percy smiled. 'Why would Adele go to the trouble of sending it if she had not wished for your company…' He paused, looked at the invitation again. 'Sorry, *our* company.' He whistled, smacked it lightly with the back of his hand, as if his name on the invitation was confirmation of its earnestness. 'It has all the details of a wedding, even if its presentation is a little less than ceremonial.'

Mary took the invitation and folded it back into the envelope, positioning it behind a statue of Eros on the mantle.

'Nevertheless, we shall not attend. As they have given no address for correspondence, I am unable to send our regrets.' Mary coughed. 'Excuse me for a moment, I just need to…'

Mary left the drawing room, exiting in the opposite direction from Claire. She felt Percy hover in the silence, unsure of which route to take next; both paths was strewn with obstacles. She had been so distant since their child's death, had he found it impossible to get through to her? Claire had been so open with her affection and her praise, but had it ever gone any further? It was a question she had never dared to ask. Hearing Percy's footsteps echoing down the hallway, she crept back into the room.

Picking up the invitation, she hesitated in front of the fire. If Claire's letter was what she expected it to be — an invitation to join a household in Piccadilly Terrace — then there would be no need to go away again. As it happened, the decision was taken out of her hands, Claire's silhouette framed the open door and Mary thrust the invitation into her pocket.

'Is this your work?' Claire's letter fluttered in her hand.

'What?' Mary swallowed.

'This sudden invitation to spend the summer as a paid companion to Lady Mawdsley. It says that *James Berry* has recommended me.'

'Well then, you have your answer. I don't know a Lady Mawdsley,' Mary could feel the heat rising to her cheeks. She had never been very good at lying, though on this occasion she was telling the truth. Their acquaintance, Doctor James Berry might have offered the solution, but Percy had sweetened the deal with a substantial contribution to Lady Mawdsley's charitable foundation.

Claire stared at Mary. 'You have your wish, you are free of me, as you always intended. If I agree to go, that is.'

'I hear Lord Byron has taken residence there.' Mary smiled. Claire's eyes flickered. Byron had always been her favourite poet, and she did so want a poet of her own.

'Yes, well, Lord Byron has also recently taken a wife, so that is no incentive,' Claire huffed. A silence fell between them as Mary waited to see if Claire would take the bait.

'Do you wish me to go?' Claire's voice trembled as she spoke.

'I want what I have always wanted for you, Claire, nothing but your happiness.'

Claire folded her arms. 'I will need to learn more about this dowager before I decide.'

'You have often talked about finding a position,' Mary countered.

'I knew this day would come, eventually.' Claire sighed. 'I did not realise it would come so quickly.' She shook her head. 'Perhaps I will seek Percy's counsel, he is always so wise when it comes to such matters. I shall go for a walk and think about it.'

'Luncheon will be served soon.'

'I'm not hungry.'

Mary listened to Claire's footsteps as she walked down the corridor towards the front door. The move to a bigger house was supposed to have given them the space they'd all desperately craved after living on top of each other at the apartment at Nelson Square, but a bigger house and circumstance had conspired to pull them in separate directions. Percy reappeared once Claire had closed the door.

'Where has she gone?'

'For a walk,' Mary replied.

'I do not understand her at all.'

'You do not need to,' Mary replied flatly.

Mary crossed to the bookcase where she picked a book and settled herself down on the settle, discarding her shoes.

'It pleases me to see you with a book, Mary. I cannot remember the last time I saw you reading.'

'I have not had the concentration for it, but I find that news of Claire's new position has freed up my imagination.' She was aware of Percy watching her, a smile creeping across his face as he watched her turn the pages.

'What?' she said, placing the book down on her knee. 'Why are you watching me?'

'I am just delighted to see you like this.' He shrugged. '*This* is the Mary I know.' He hesitated. 'I overheard you and Clara.'

Mary caught her breath. It was the name of her daughter, not her sister's nickname. She had almost forgotten that Percy had once called her that.

'She is to be a paid companion? A perfect role for her, one she has been perfecting these past twelve months. Will she need references?'

'I am sure a recommendation from the great poet Percy Shelley would be more than sufficient.' Mary picked up the book and resumed reading, before looking up again. 'Be sure to mention that she is prone to shifting affections, jealousy, acts of vandalism and melancholy, will you?'

A shocked laugh burst from Percy. 'Mary, you can dissect a personality right back to its marrow. Anyway, I do believe —' Percy cast uncertain eyes around the room before edging closer to the settle, where he perched himself and leant towards Mary — 'our friend Dr Berry has already seen to the references. It is a friend of one of his relatives,' he whispered.

'Is that so?' A smile crept across Mary's face. 'Is there no end to his usefulness?'

'It would appear not.' Percy pulled out his pocket watch. 'I am starving.' His stomach rumbled in confirmation. 'Luncheon will be served presently. Will you dine?'

'I will feast on words, Percy. But perhaps some soup and bread might be saved for later? I am sure to be ravenous when I've finished this folio.'

'Right.' Percy bowed his head and left the room.

Percy felt swallowed up by the vast table of which he was the head; it seemed to stretch out for miles in front of him, laden with all the expected finery of his social status, yet his heart ached for simpler times, when he and Mary and Claire had all lived and cooked together in one small space. He could never get all the elements of his life working in harmony: now his grandfather had finally raised his allowance and pulled them out of their winter of poverty, this house should have heralded a new start — a new daughter, a home, a place where love and creativity would dance together like spring flowers, but it had not been like that. Since the baby's death, Mary had been plunged into an endless winter whose chill fog had crept through all the spaces of the house, enveloping them all. He had scraped words out of his misery, but the effort had taken its toll and he felt exhausted. The only person who greeted him at the dining table was his reflection in the vase, and even then his features were so contorted as to be almost unrecognisable.

Percy pulled at a bread roll until it was nothing but crumbs; only then did he put it in his mouth, chewing on it slowly and laboriously as if it were stone. His cheekbones pushed against the skin as he chewed; he was disappearing, drowning in the reflected waters of Mary's grief and there were only so many times he could pull himself out.

'I'm not too late, am I?' Claire's flushed cheeks sparked a reluctant fire in Percy. It was only at such moments that he fully realised how lonely he was, how starved of company.

'I cannot get used to dining at specific times, we spent so long snatching at biscuits and pretending not to be hungry that I have almost forgotten what a dining table is.'

Percy smiled and indicated a chair. 'Sit down, Claire.'

'What flavour is the soup today? What delights are boiled in the broth?' Claire's eyes twinkled. 'Is it meat?'

'Don't be impertinent,' replied Percy, an ardent vegetarian. 'You know very well the only animal in our kitchen is the kitchen cat. The soup is celery...' He hesitated, circled his spoon around the bowl. 'I think.'

'It is certainly the colour of celery. Most verdant.' Claire picked up her spoon. 'Well, Percy, you will be delighted to know that I have made my decision.'

'Decision?' It took him a moment to comprehend what she was talking about.

Claire nodded. 'Yes, about a position I have been offered with Lady Mawdsley. Actually, this soup is quite agreeable. I have more of a hunger than I'd realised.' She tore at the bread.

'And are we to know what your decision is?'

Claire pointed a piece of bread at him and carried on chewing. Hours seemed to pass until she had finished masticating. 'You know full well what my decision is — it is not as though I have a choice in the matter.'

'You are a free individual, Claire, you have nothing *but* choice.'

'Really? Well, let us not resume our debate on the philosophy of choice for a woman who dares to shun the demands of her social class, the food will go cold before we agree on that point.' She straightened her shoulders. 'But I have decided and I think it would be best for us all if I accept the position.'

'You will be missed.' Percy hadn't realised that he'd finished the soup and the bread; nothing restored his appetite like good news.

'By you, perhaps, but not by Mary.'

'Mary has found it hard to come to terms with her loss.'

The words felt bitter on his tongue. It was his loss too, but he purged his grief on paper.

'She has been like a ghost.' Claire looked down at the bowl, as if the past were reflected there. 'It has been a difficult time for us all.'

'It has, but I hope that our adventure to Salt Hill has restored something of her old spark. She said she did not wish to eat because she wanted to finish her book. I cannot recall the last time I saw her reading.'

'I cannot recall the last time I saw her do anything other than stare into space.'

'She is healing, I am sure of it.' Percy swallowed, not meeting Claire's gaze in case she saw the uncertainty in his own.

'I hope you are right, there are ghosts enough in this house without adding another to their ranks.'

Claire and Percy laughed through the remaining courses, unaware of the phantom figure that hovered briefly at the door. Mary smiled to herself. It had been a good idea to implore James to use his contacts to find Claire a position, and even better to make Percy believe it had all been his own doing. Mary made her way silently back to the drawing room.

CHAPTER TWO

Being back in London reminded Claire how much she'd missed it; the ebb and flow of activity, the surprising pockets of greenery hidden beyond the facades of houses and shops, the sound of horses' hooves on the cobbled streets as carts and carriages rushed by. Even the smell of the city's air that fused soil, chemicals and rotting vegetables was pleasant to her — it meant there was evidence of life; everything was dead in Bishopsgate.

The carriage pulled up outside a terrace of dazzling white houses complemented by the green open space of the opposite park. Claire shuddered, reminded of the crime she had witnessed in a similar place. She picked up her bag and took a deep breath. Her heart was pounding and her throat was dry as she walked down the road. Byron and his new wife lived in this row too; she was unsure of the number but it would be easy enough to uncover now she was living here. Perhaps Lady Mawdsley had made their acquaintance and they would be regular visitors at the house. If Claire were ever to make his acquaintance — and she was determined it was only *his* acquaintance she sought — she would not be presented as a paid companion, she would be his equal.

As she walked, Claire took in the perfect columns, which seemed shorn from the same white stone as the houses. The artistic iron curls at the end of the railing were a relief, splayed out like peacock feathers, obscuring the number of the house behind it. Maybe this was his? Byron was sure to put his own theatrical stamp on a house — conventionality seemed only to be used to mask his divergence from it. Claire hesitated outside the house, half hoping that Lady Byron would run out in a rage, determined to leave her brute of a husband once and for all. Wouldn't that be exquisite timing for Claire to be on the doorstep, ready to console him? It wasn't as if she hadn't much experience dealing with temperamental poets. Percy was really very easy-going, but he was not in Byron's league in terms of reputation or published works. An acquaintance with Byron would be a good thing for them all. Claire smiled. Her external motives might be altruistic, but her inner desires were anything but. She hadn't noticed she'd been staring up at the house until she saw the figure of a servant staring back at her. Flushed, she put her head down and hurried on.

Lady Mawdsley's house was at the end of Piccadilly Terrace, at the opposite end of the iron railing. So little distance between them. Claire tried to stop the fireworks of fantasy sparking in her imagination, but as it had been the only reason she had accepted the position, they were hard to extinguish. Adopting a professional air, she made her way up the steps to the front door. A servant answered her knock. She wore an identical black uniform to the servant she'd seen in the other window — was it possible that the woman had merely run from one house into the other? What fun that would be, if all the houses on the terrace were connected, what delightful trouble that could cause.

'Yes? What is it?'

The lack of manners made Claire pause.

'I am expected by Lady Mawdsley. I am the new companion.'

The woman raised her eyebrows. 'You'd better come in then. Be prepared to duck.'

Claire frowned. 'Duck?' As she entered, a tomato skimmed past Claire's head before splattering on the ground.

'I told you.' The other woman's head was lowered. 'Keep your head down until you see if she's got anything else in her hand.'

'Anything else?' Claire stammered. What sort of lady threw vegetables?

'Is this the new Claire?' a stentorian voice boomed through the building. Lady Mawdsley clearly had powerful lungs as well as a powerful throw.

'The *new* Claire?' Claire asked the servant.

'All her companions are called Claire, just as all her husbands were called Ernest — makes it easier to remember them, or easier to forget.'

'I don't pay you to stand around all day. I pay you to look after me. Bring the new Claire to me this instant!' Lady Mawdsley's voice boomed again.

'Right away, ma'am,' the servant called. Then, to Claire, 'I'm Pearl,' she whispered.

'Claire Clairmont.' As their heads were already bowed, they nodded to each other in place of any other courtesies.

Pearl pushed the front door closed behind them, keeping her body low as she moved. Claire stood upright, smoothed down her gown and plastered on a smile.

'I heard she once threw a sheep at a farmer who wouldn't let her walk through his field.' Pearl shook her head in astonishment. 'I wouldn't put it past her.'

An apple brushed past Claire's cheek, knocking down a statue of a Greek god.

'Clear that up, Pearl, and come here, Claire.'

Claire walked tentatively past the maimed statue, whose head had been successfully sliced from its body. She gulped down her fears, reminding herself that she needed a break from Mary and Percy as much as they needed a break from her; she just hoped she'd come out of it in one piece.

Lady Mawdsley sat in a red chair, her eyes closed, bathed in the golden sunshine that shone through the window. Her profile reminded Claire of the portraits of kings and queens. Her long straight nose met the sharp jawline, her silver hair was piled on her head as if awaiting a crown. At her neck, an elaborate necklace of night-sky sapphires shimmered. She wasn't just a woman; she was a force of nature. Opening one eye, she turned towards Claire.

'There you are!' she said, as if the apple and tomato had been fragments of Claire's imagination. Lady Mawdsley held out a long, graceful hand, weighed down by a sapphire the size of a pebble. 'I am Lady Edna Mawdsley, widow of Sir Ernest Mawdsley. You may have heard of him?'

Claire hadn't, but nodded all the same.

'You are the *infamous* Claire Clairmont.' The old lady's eyes sparkled as she leant forward.

'I wouldn't call myself *infamous*...' Claire began. Lady Mawdsley held up her hand to silence her.

'The *infamous* never do. It is not for you to label yourself, it is for society to tell you who you are.' Lady Mawdsley sat back and closed her eyes again, her wisdom imparted. 'Luckily for you I do not listen to the tittle-tattle of society; I prefer to surround myself with interesting people. Tell me, Claire, are you an interesting person?'

'I can speak French and Latin and play the piano,' Claire offered. Now she was roll calling her achievements, they didn't sound that impressive.

'And that will get you two thousand a year and a clergy husband with gout.' Lady Mawdsley waved her hand. 'No, that is not what makes a person interesting. Your stepsister ran off with Percy Shelley, did she not? She being the daughter of Mary Wollstonecraft, who ran off to Paris, did she not?'

'That she is, and that she did.' Claire frowned, she was already being out-danced by the old lady's grammar.

'Fascinating.' Lady Mawdsley sighed. 'You absconded to Paris?'

'I wouldn't say absconded...'

That hand again, punctuating Claire's sentences, telling Claire that Lady Mawdsley would not be corrected.

'We went to Paris, Switzerland and Germany.'

'And you still came back to London?' Lady Mawdsley shook her head, the jewels twinkling in sympathy. 'I too have undertaken a grand tour — several, in fact. I am planning one to Geneva next year, there is already talk of it, I just need to detach Lady Byron from the idea.' She pursed her lips. 'Do you know the Byrons?'

Claire's heart thudded. How best to answer this? Confessing her genuine desires and intentions would make her look like a love-struck schoolgirl of nothing but whim and fancy, when her actual intentions had much longer-lasting implications.

'No, I do not. I have read Lord Byron's poetry, of course.'

'Most of the world has read his poetry.' Lady Mawdsley sniffed. 'I do not care for it much myself. It is too ... too...' She paused, searching for the word. 'Boyish,' she settled on at last.

'And does the man match the poetry?' Claire asked.

Lady Mawdsley slapped her hand on her knee, her shoulders hunched in a sudden defiant expression, matched by a scowl that bit her features.

'What an impertinent question to ask,' she snapped, fidgeting in the chair as if suddenly besieged by an itch. A sure sign —

Claire realised — that Claire had stepped out of the invisible socially acceptable parameters that surrounded her.

The mood in the room seemed to change; the sun disappeared behind a cloud as shadows danced over the room's artefacts like sudden ghosts.

'Pearl!' Lady Mawdsley boomed, her features settling back into their patrician form. 'Pearl!'

Claire winced as Lady Mawdsley screeched into the air. Pearl quickly appeared and the old lady settled again — not only a force of nature, a tempest.

'Yes, m'lady?'

'Tea for myself and Claire, and have her bags taken to her quarters.' She turned to Claire. 'Your room is next to mine, in case I need you during the evening. You needn't worry, I am not expecting you to help with ablutions or such matters, but if I cannot settle I may ask you to read to me, poetry perhaps, though not George's.' She shook her head gravely. 'I have been invited to visit my friends in Shropshire in August. You will accompany me if your trial goes well.'

'Trial?' Claire asked.

Pearl laid the tea things in front of Claire, their eyes met briefly, and Claire saw the flicker of a smile curling at Pearl's lip.

'We have to see if we are compatible. If I can tolerate you.' Lady Mawdsley gestured for Pearl to pour the tea. The servant sprang into action on receipt of the command. Like a well-trained dog, Claire thought. In her mind, it wasn't so much the case of whether or not Lady Mawdsley could tolerate *her*, but how long *she* could tolerate Lady Mawdsley. Her heart ached for Mary and Percy and the pull of their domestic life weighed heavily on her, The bonfire that was supposed to allow them all to move on, had severed them entirely. If only she could extinguish her jealousy. Perhaps a tenure with Lady Mawdsley would sort that.

'You drink your tea like a lady of breeding. That is a good start. This afternoon we will take a stroll in the park. You will push my three wheel, it will be no effort for you.'

Claire frowned. If Lady Mawdsley could not walk, how had she managed to throw a tomato out of the door or an apple into the hallway? She certainly was an enigmatic woman.

'I am mobile, but I like to conserve my energy where possible. As it is one of your duties, you will push me. I had it shipped in from Paris. It is the only one of its kind in London.' Lady Mawdsley stretched up, a proud peacock displaying its feathers.

'I have never pushed one before, I feel a little anxious about it.'

'Persephone!' Lady Mawdsley's voice sang, suddenly higher pitched and more melodious than before. A small, short-legged dog scampered across the floor, brushing Claire's legs as it passed.

'I presume you have no problem with animals? This is my Skye Terrier, Persephone. Walking her will be part of your duties as well. Perhaps the two of you can get acquainted. She does so enjoy a turn in the three wheel.'

'You want me to wheel the dog around the park?' Claire asked, failing to keep the surprise from her voice.

'You said you needed the practise. You can either experiment with darling Persephone or with me.' Lady Mawdsley turned her steely gaze towards Claire, menace hovered just below the surface. 'Which is it to be?'

'Have I time to finish my tea first?' Claire gulped.

'Of course! I am not an ogre, despite appearances.' Lady Mawdsley clapped her hands together, laughing at the mere idea of it. Persephone barked through a face obscured entirely by hair, the shade of which almost matched Lady Mawdsley's own grey hair. 'Finish your tea quickly; as soon as Persephone hears the word *walk*, she gets excited, don't you darling?'

The dog barked in agreement. Lady Mawdsley's features softened as she spoke to the dog; she looked more kindly, like a beloved grandmother rather than a harsh matriarch. How quickly and easily she could flutter between these two extremes; what a formidable young woman she must have been. It was no wonder she'd been married and widowed three times. Claire couldn't imagine that any man could keep pace with her — even now. Claire put the cup down.

'Now we have made our acquaintances and Pearl has taken your belongings to your quarters, you will take Persephone for her promenade and I will rest. It is always exhausting to meet new people.'

Claire stood up, nodded, and motioned for the dog. It was no good, there was no way Persephone could see anything beneath all that hair, which fell from the top of her head down to her paws like a giant curtain. Just as well the dog was to travel in the three wheel; how could it possibly see where it was going to navigate the streets of London?

'Pearl!' Lady Mawdsley bellowed again. 'Pearl, come and help Miss Clairmont with the three wheel.'

'Come along, Persephone.' Claire mimicked the bright, lofty tone of Lady Mawdsley's command and the dog walked towards her. Pearl wheeled the chair into position.

Claire picked up the dog.

'Here we go, Persephone,' she said as she placed the dog on the seat. Its hair divided in the middle, showing a pair of unimpressed black eyes gazing up at her with an appropriate level of suspicion. 'Perhaps she would benefit from a blanket or a cushion?' The words left Claire's mouth before she realised what she'd even said.

Lady Mawdsley smiled. 'An excellent point, Claire. I can see you have already fallen for Persephone's charms. Pearl, a cushion.'

Pearl appeared with a velvet cushion, which she tucked under the dog with no fuss. Persephone sat atop it like a prize.

'That is much better.' Lady Mawdsley nodded and turned her face back towards the sun, which had reappeared. Pearl opened the front door.

The row of steps that had seemed so grand and inviting on the way in, now looked like an insurmountable obstacle.

'How are we going to get down those steps?' Claire whispered.

'It's much easier with Persephone than with Lady Mawdsley. Bump Lady Mawdsley and you'll be looking for another job.'

Claire had to admit that was a tempting proposition.

'I'll take the front wheel, you hold on to the back.'

'Right.' Claire nodded.

They navigated the dog down the steps, stopping to wish a passing couple a good morning and trying to ignore the bemused glance they gave as they passed. Claire didn't want to think about how this looked, two grown women taking a dog down the stairs like Cleopatra on her throne. Thoughts of Mary and Percy knotted her stomach again; if only she had been kinder and more considerate to Mary, then she wouldn't have been ostracised from their inner circle and be here now, about to push a Skye Terrier called Persephone around a park like an infant.

'Here goes.' Claire took a deep breath, gritted her teeth, and pushed.

*

Mary had been reading the same chapter for a month. Though she'd tried to immerse herself back into her previous regime of literature and learning, she had found the literature part easier than the learning; the Greek verbs danced before her eyes, refusing to conjugate or transform themselves into the expected participles. She rubbed her eyes and yawned; there was no point getting stressed about it. Percy was out on one of his London errands and her sighs rang hollow on the house's deaf ears. At times like this she would normally seek Claire out. The mere fact of having another person with her — even one who inspired a constantly quelled anger like she did — would be reassuring. She didn't miss her, exactly, but she missed the idea of company and the grief was only too willing to accompany her loneliness.

Mary looked out of the window onto banks of green trees that edged the water like a patient crowd. She wondered if she might bring herself to take a stroll. Last winter, before the baby's birth, she had done nothing but walk around, finding solace in the escape from their oppressive lodgings; determined that the baby should feel life, light and air, so it would not be too much of a shock when she came into the world. She would walk the London streets, watching the busy people, feeling the sharp slap of the winter breeze on her cheeks, the slow mist that clung to her hair and dress. She'd had so many dreams then, visions of walking with her daughter, laughing at people desperately trying to stay upright on the sheets of ice that blanketed the streets. Mary had imagined her daughter's hand holding on to hers, hot as a pebble. She couldn't bear to take a stroll now.

Putting down the book, she swallowed the lump in her throat. At least she could stop the tears now, that something. She stretched out her arms and legs, the delicious pull of her muscles reminding her she wasn't just a shell, that her body was still there and working. Taking a deep breath, her nostrils caught the scent of the flowers Percy had brought in from the garden; such a ramshackle, homespun collection. He'd presented them to her like a proud child. Their scent was overpowering, suffused with the remnants of their birth, the wet soil clinging to the odour. Mary rushed from the settle, making it to the chamber pot before a tidal wave of vomit rushed from her. She stared, her mouth open in disbelief. They had only resumed their intimacy recently. She could not possibly be pregnant again, could she? Was her body to put her through all this pain again? Mary sleepwalked the bowl through the house, out of the back door towards the stream, her mind as full and heavy as the bowl's contents. She walked carefully, holding the bowl in outstretched arms, but its acid smell still burned the back of her nostrils. This was a cruel trick of nature. Just as the mind was laying to rest the winter of her daughter's birth and death, her body was resurrecting her. It would be a boy this time. Her heart would not stand another girl.

'Mary? Mary, are you here?' Percy's voice danced through the open door. Mary was glad that it was the servants' day off, so there had been no witnesses. Having disposed of the bowl's contents, she sloshed it in the water, apologising to its inhabitants for the intrusion, then dropped the bowl by the tree and hurried back to the house.

'Sorry, Percy, I was outside. I thought I heard a trapped bird.' A trapped bird in the garden? Oh dear, she really needed to work on her spontaneous excuses.

Percy's features creased with concern. 'And did you find anything?'

'No, I did not. I think the other birds must have come back for it.' Great, now she'd added a family to the story.

'We can only presume the tale has a happy ending.' Percy gave a self-gratified giggle. 'Tale? Tail? Bird's tail feathers?'

'Oh yes, very good Percy.' Mary patted him on the shoulder. She was unusually slow to get the joke, being — as she was — preoccupied with her own affairs.

'Are you well, Mary? You seem a little out of sorts.'

Panic flared through her body, before resting like a heavy stone in her stomach.

'Yes, Percy, I am well. Perhaps I am a little skittish today, my mind dances and I have found it hard to concentrate on my Greek verbs.'

Talk of Greek and Latin always threw him off subject; Mary knew that mentioning it was a shortcut back to the hideous classrooms of Percy's youth.

'You are a better scholar than I, Mary.' He pulled her to him and kissed the top of her head. Mary closed her eyes, enjoying the brief glow of affection. She put her arms around him.

'What the...?' Percy strained his head past Mary. 'Why is that duck sniffing a chamber pot? Isn't that one of ours?'

Mary followed Percy's gaze towards the incessant quacking. There had been no ducks ten minutes earlier.

'I believe it to be mine.' Mary extracted herself from Percy's embrace.

'Careful.' Percy held her arm. 'Ducks bite.'

'I am sure you are confusing them with geese, Percy. I mean only to extract the chamber pot, not harm the creature.'

'It seems reluctant to part with it.'

Percy was right, the duck was pecking at the upturned chamber pot with a persistent beak, desperate to appraise its contents. It was a good job she'd washed it; what a hideous discovery it would be otherwise.

'What should we do?' Mary whispered.

'The duck will lose interest soon enough. Let us go inside, I have a surprise for you!'

'Do you like it?'

Mary held the dress in front of her. It was more elaborate than her usual style and felt heavy and pretentious. She knew the brocade was very much of the season, but as she cared more for comfort than style, it was hard to picture herself in it without thinking of it as some kind of performance, as if she were a small child trying on its mother's clothes. The yellow silk was supposed to remind her of summer daffodils and sunshine, but it turned her stomach.

'There are matching shoes, gloves and reticule!' Percy added with delight.

Mary found it hard to match his enthusiasm and wondered how he had been talked into such a monstrosity. Ordinarily, she'd have cursed Claire for this abomination, but for once Claire was not to blame — unless Percy had secretly met up with her in London? That would not be out of the realm of possibility. An uneasy feeling possessed her.

'Mary? You've gone pale.'

Percy's words floated away as both she and the dress fell to the floor in a heap. When she came to, she hoped Percy would not remember how frequently she had fainted in early pregnancy with Clara.

'It must have been the excitement of the gown.' She smiled and Percy smiled back.

'You might wish to stay on the floor then, Mary, for there is a reason for the new dress. I accepted the invitation to Adele's wedding.' Percy clapped his hands together with an enthusiasm Mary found difficult to emulate; how dare he respond to her wedding invitation! Irritation pushed nausea aside and Mary sat up, leaving the dress on the floor.

'I told you I did not wish to attend Adele's wedding!'

'There is no point holding on to grievances, Mary. It will be good for you to clear the air.'

Mary stared at him. The temptation to recall the many instances where she'd had to soothe, placate or barter with people Percy had upset was on the tip of her tongue. She swallowed them down.

Percy's eyes shone with excitement. Sometimes he could be spectacularly slow at reading her reaction to things. 'A beautiful gown for a beautiful wedding guest. I have arranged rooms at the local inn — we leave this afternoon.'

'This afternoon?' Mary cried.

'Adele is overjoyed that we are attending the wedding, she is greatly looking forward to renewing your acquaintance.'

'How did you even get in touch with her?'

'I sent a letter to the local church.'

Mary gaped. There was no changing Percy's mind when he settled on something. No matter what she said now, she could not convince him that this was anything other than wonderful.

'How long are we going for?'

'We will get there this evening,' Percy started. 'We will stay for the wedding and the following weekend, then travel back on Monday.'

'We will be gone for almost a week?' There was no way she could hide the sickness that long. If it *was* pregnancy sickness. Perhaps it was nothing more than a reaction to something she ate — though that was unlikely given their diet contained no meat, milk or sugar. Percy had given that up in solidarity with the plantation workers. She would hope that it was a stomach upset or, at least, pretend that it was. The advantage of Percy's boundless optimism was that he was quite naïve and believed everything he was told. It *would* be nice to see Adele again, though she could only hope that her choice of husband was better than Lilian's. She shuddered. If she convinced herself that she wouldn't see Reginald, knowing he'd forbid Lilian attending if he knew they were invited, then she could allow herself to focus on the positive aspects — a wedding was always a joyful affair and Adele the sweetest and most mild-mannered of women. She was sure that Adele and Percy would get on famously; their temperaments were very similar. Adele loved animals, art and literature, and would spend lessons drawing pictures of squirrels, sighing and daydreaming as she recited cantos from *Childe Harold*. It was possible that Mary had only been invited to the wedding *because* of her relationship with Shelley; for the notoriety of it. That really would be a first, and it wasn't as though their social calendar was bursting at the seams. The move to Windsor had been a reaction to being the subject of London's gossips and an attempt to put some distance between themselves and the grave-robbing gang they'd sent to the gallows.

Mary sighed. 'What time does our carriage leave?'

CHAPTER THREE

'And are you sure this is the right church this time?' Mary
gritted her teeth. So far, they had interrupted one baptism, one
burial and precisely no weddings. She was sticky and agitated,
the carriage was stifling and the window only let the smallest
breath of air in. At least it was a private carriage, which was its
only consolation.

The journey had taken two days and there were many points
during it that Mary suspected that the only church service she
would attend was her own funeral. Percy, whose philosophical
leanings had made him question any sort of divine figure and
resolve not to worship any until he had seen the proof of their
existence, had shown infinitely more patience and confidence
in the driver's abilities.

'You cannot deny that we have had a splendid tour of the
shires,' Percy responded, ever the optimist.

Mary's head swam with disorientation, she didn't know
whether she was coming or going. They had made several
stops — mainly for the driver to ask directions — and these
had offered welcome respite and opportunities to consume
food and regurgitate it away from Percy's inquisitive eye. The
regularity of the sickness was easy to disguise as motion
sickness, he knew all too well how poor a traveller she was; but
he had not yet made the connection between long journeys and
early pregnancy. It was a conversation for another day and one
she could not bring herself to consider yet.

'It is all very green and pleasant,' she replied. *And dull*, she
thought to herself. Everything looked the same, from the trees
to the farmers to the cows, there was nothing to distinguish

one from the other. If she didn't know better, she would have thought they had done a complete circle and simply repeated the same stretch of road *ad infinitum*. 'What time is the wedding?' she asked, half hoping they had missed it already and could turn the carriage round and go home.

'Midday,' Percy replied, taking the invitation from his pocket and checking it. He pulled out a shiny, golden pocket watch. 'We have plenty of time yet.'

Mary's chest tightened. It was difficult to know what to be more vexed about; Percy's stealing the invitation and replying to it, his organisation of this trip or his purchase of a gaudy, gold pocket watch. These weren't the actions of a mournful man. It was perfectly reasonable to be bothered by all three. The gold reflection bounced off her tired gown and she dusted it down with awkward fingers, suddenly aware of the faded ripples that adorned it. She sighed, bored with the journey and desperate to get the event over and done with. If the driver's latest predictions were to prove accurate, they were only a couple of leagues from their destination, but she had stopped trusting him after the first wrong turning of the journey and they had found themselves in a ditch in Hampshire.

'Shall I read to you to pass the time?' Percy asked. He'd already retrieved the small red book from his breast pocket, so the question was really a politeness.

'That would be lovely.' Mary sighed. 'I may close my eyes to fully appreciate the words.'

Percy's soft voice was made for Shakespeare's sonnets. Mary felt all her previous anxieties float away as the sunlight beamed through the carriage window and onto her face, warming her through, soothing her, wanting her to heal. Her mind wandered, allowing itself a brief glimpse of the future they would have had with their daughter; she saw them in a golden cornfield on a summer's day, gazing upon Clara as if she were the most precious jewel on earth. For a moment, love flooded through her body, wrapping her in the sensation and holding her there tightly. Until she noticed a dark spot in the distance, a small stain that crept through the cornfield like an inkblot, growing in size and confidence until it revealed itself to be a monstrous crow the size of a human. Mary was frozen by horror as the crow swept towards the child, pecking at her dress with a beak as big as a hand before carrying the child away into the sun. Mary's scream pierced through the vision, waking her up with an abrupt start.

'Mary?' Percy whispered, clasping her hand. 'Did you have a nightmare?'

She shook her head, giving herself time for the thoughts to evaporate before speaking. 'No, I was daydreaming, but the vision turned just as the seasons do.' She stretched, hissing at the sharp pain at the base of her spine. Percy bumbled around her, she batted him away with quick hands.

'I am fine, I am fine,' she repeated. Eventually, he took the hint and retreated into the seat, but concern creased his brow. He opened his mouth as if to speak, then closed it again. Mary was glad of the reprieve and took a few deep breaths through her nose, letting the air escape slowly through her mouth, until she was sure that the pain had subsided — all of them.

'I must have moved myself awkwardly as I slept. I twinged my back, nothing more. How long have I slept?'

'You should not ask how long, but how far, for we are almost there. Can you not hear the church bells?'

Mary frowned. No, she couldn't hear anything. Percy erupted with laughter. She tapped him lightly on the arm.

'You do so like to make fun of me. I can scarcely tell when you are being serious.'

'We *are* almost there, I was not joking about that.'

'Will there be time to change my outfit before the wedding?' She blushed at the thought of arriving at the wedding in this state.

'I shall ask the driver.' Percy banged on the roof of the carriage, the horses neighed and whinnied before the carriage drew to a halt.

'Yes?' The driver opened the door, his voice as weary as his face.

'How much longer until we arrive at the church?'

'We will get there a lot faster if I don't need to stop the horses to answer your questions, sir.' The driver removed the hat from his head and scratched his head. The sight of his black hair stuck to his forehead made Mary's stomach turn, reminding her of the smell of sweat — even if his distance from her thankfully prevented a closer acquaintance. 'Reckon about fifteen minutes, it shouldn't be far now.'

'Is there somewhere on route that I can change?' Mary leant forward and instantly regretted it as the sweet sweat climbed into her nostrils.

'There's a turning, an enclosed woodland with a lake, you could go there?'

'Mary! It will be like being back in Paris!' Percy's eyes widened, and he grabbed her arm. Mary frowned, how interchangeable the sisters must have been for him to misremember it so.

'You are mistaken, Percy. I did not frolic in the lake in Paris. That was Claire.'

'Either way,' said Percy, waving his hand in the air, 'at least you have the option of changing your gown. It does not matter to me if you wear this dress or the lemon gown; whatever makes you most comfortable, or helps you make the best impression.'

'I have no desire to make any sort of impression at all.' Mary folded her arms, remembering that she had never intended to go to the wedding and suddenly feeling very bitter about it. She could be at home, resting on the settle, reading poetry.

'I know you are anxious about seeing certain people again, but I will be with you…'

She didn't have the heart to tell him he was the reason dear Lilian had severed all ties with her — or been forced to sever them.

'I am not feeling anxious, though it is sweet of you to leap to my defence.' Mary smiled and patted his hand. 'I am expecting awkwardness, for I have not seen Lilian for two years and that feels like a lifetime.' She sighed. 'So much has happened, I scarcely recognise the girl I was then, I do not feel I have anything in common with her. I cannot remember her mannerisms or her smile, her topics of conversation or ideas. If I am anxious about anything, it is how to resurrect myself so I may resemble the Mary she remembers. For she is the one Lilian invited to the wedding, not I.'

'You are not so very changed, my dear.' Percy kissed her hand. 'I see the girl I met at William Godwin's table; you had not long returned from Scotland then. I see no difference between the two. Your experiences may have altered you in your own eyes, but not in mine.'

The driver coughed. 'Are we stopping at the lake, then?'

Mary and Percy tipped their heads together, giggling at the driver's reprimanding tone. Mary nodded, and the driver walked back to the front of the carriage, shaking his head as he went. Slowly, the layers of winter were peeling back and the icy chill that had imprisoned her heart was thawing and remembering some of its former feeling. Gratitude illuminated her, and she remembered that despite everything the shadows had told her, she was not alone.

True to the driver's word, they arrived at the lake moments later and Percy helped Mary out of the travelling gown and into the yellow one; as he helped to tie the bodice at the back, the sensation of his fingers weaving through the laces made her skin tingle. He had just navigated the bow at the bottom of the bodice when the driver's whistle bounced through the trees.

'If you want to make it in time, you need to get back in the carriage.'

Percy rested his hand on Mary's shoulder, she put her own atop it and closed her eyes; wishing to suspend time for a moment and cling to this feeling of togetherness, but the moment was soon broken by the sound of a horse breaking wind in the distance.

'That's a countryside bugle.' Percy smiled. 'Come on, you look beautiful.'

He held her hand back to the carriage, and as they walked, Mary allowed herself to be swept along with the fantasy of this being their wedding day; that the gown and the celebrations were for them; but that could never be, it did not matter how long they lived together nor how many children she bore, Harriet was Percy's wife in the eyes of the law and her children were alive and well, unlike her own. The thought sent a spidery chill creeping up her neck. Mary put a hand to her stomach, snatching it away when Percy turned to look at her.

Mary forced herself to smile, but Percy's face creased for a moment, and she knew he was trying to decipher her actions. She stepped back into the carriage, this dress was more voluminous than the previous one and it forced Percy to sit on the opposite seat.

'I doubt the bride will be as beautiful as you.' His gaze — like his words — were sincere and the smile that returned them was genuine, but the word *bride* fell upon her like an unexpected blow. She had not realised that not being Percy's wife bothered her so much.

'Is that them?' Percy whispered as the figures of a man in morning dress and a woman dressed in a bridal cap and gown exited the church. As it had been a couple of years since she had seen Adele, her recollections were hazy.

'I do not know.' Mary shrugged. 'Perhaps we are too early and have interrupted someone else's party. Oh...'

She hesitated. She might not place Adele and her new husband, but there was no mistaking Reginald Ullmann. Mary shuddered. Even the thought of being close to him made her skin crawl. Now they had certain confirmation of his presence at the wedding, Mary wanted to turn back to the carriage and drive home.

'Is that him?' Percy whispered, leaning towards her.

'If you mean that indomitable brute with no scruples, otherwise known as Reginald Ullmann, then you are correct.' Mary clutched Percy's arm. 'I was hoping he would not be here, but I see it was too much to ask.'

'At least you will get to speak to Lilian, that will be some consolation?'

'If he allows it.' Mary tutted. 'You know his viewpoint on fallen women.'

'His own morality is questionable,' Percy admitted. 'Though I do not pretend to talk from personal experience. Quick!'

Percy pulled them towards a memorial stone shaped like a winged angel, situated to the right of the church; they waited there as the happy procession passed with vaguely remembered faces and much fanfare. A swarm of well-wishers perched themselves on the stone wall, the women cupping their faces with their hands or trying to attract the attention of their disinterested men. The vicar walked past, a kindly faced elderly man who laughed as he spoke.

'My final wedding.' The vicar smiled at Mary. 'What a wondrous event to end on. I suppose I shall have to get the church affairs in order.' He shook his head and walked on. Lilian walked past and the sight of her made Mary gasp, Lilian turned at the noise and Mary shrank back, clasping at the stone for purchase before tumbling onto the ground.

'Mary?'

Percy raced to the side of the ornament she had tumbled behind, helping her up from of the grass.

Mary could do nothing but stare. It was as though every grain of youth had been sucked out of Lilian, leaving her nothing but a husk of her former self. Her brown hair was threaded with premature grey, her skin the colour of gruel, and the shadows under her eyes were longer than the shadows cast by a bright summer's day; only the voice gave her away.

'Lilian, why are you talking to a statue?' Reginald's brisk voice boomed out. Mary watched her friend prickle at the sound, like a hedgehog preparing its spikes.

'Oh.' His expression soured as he noticed Mary. 'So, they *were* invited?' He spat the words in Lilian's direction, his back towards Mary and Percy.

'It would appear so. Isn't it lovely to reunite for an occasion like this?'

'We will miss the wedding breakfast if you insist on this idle chatter. Come along.'

He grabbed Lilian's arm and started pulling her along. Percy dived forward, but Mary shook her head and he retreated.

'Not so much as an introduction or a politeness,' Percy stammered. 'What an exceptionally rude man.'

'I told you.' Mary shrugged. Reginald wasn't worth the breath of saying more. 'Do not let Reginald's ill manners spoil the day. I have a new dress, you are looking most handsome; if we are to be talked about, at least let them talk of our impeccable manners and fine dress.'

They walked to the wedding breakfast housed in a charming stone building off the village green. It had been decked with brightly coloured flags and sprigs of spring flowers that rested next to explosions of lavender, which attracted a host of extra guests — the always-welcome red admirals and cabbage white butterflies. Adele floated around the room, positively glowing, and when she spotted Mary and Percy, she broke free of the conversation and bounded over to them.

'Mary!' She threw her arms around her. Mary staggered back but accepted the gesture. Once she was extracted from Adele's enthusiastic arms, she introduced Percy.

'The poet!' Adele's eyes lit up. 'We should have commissioned a verse to celebrate our wedding. What a shame I didn't think of that before.'

Mary, who remembered all too well the last off-the-cuff poem Percy had performed and how he'd sulked at the laughter it had created, shook her head.

'Poetry is an art for Percy, he has to let the idea come to him and then work it into shape, like a sculptor.'

'It's so very kind of you to come. Have you seen Lilian and Reginald? They are here as well.'

Mary clenched her jaw. 'Yes, we have seen them. How good of them to come all the way from Dundee.'

'Oh!' Adele giggled, her voice floating up like one of the butterflies. 'They moved to Doddingley. Reginald and my husband Donald are very important people now, they own most of the land there.' She waved her hand in the air. 'They simply love playing lords of the manor.'

Percy blushed, as he did at any mention of titles and nobility; he had spent a lifetime trying to forget his. *How strange*, Mary thought, *that so many men should seek the thing that Percy tries his best to hide; how foolish society is.*

'And your father, did he move to Doddingley with you?'

At this, a shadow passed over Adele's face.

'I'm afraid my father died last year.'

'My apologies, I am sorry to hear that.' Mary's heart went out to her as she remembered the old man from visits in her childhood — red-cheeked, jovial and always so full of life — what a tragedy that he was not here to share in his daughter's happiness.

'Thank you, Mary.' Adele put her hand on Mary's, removing it quickly to dab at her eyes. 'Tears! I promised myself there would only be happy tears today.'

'He would be proud of you today.' Mary smiled. 'I'm sure he knew you'd be in safe hands with Donald.'

Adele sighed. 'Alas no, Donald didn't come into my life until my father had sadly left it. Speaking of Donald, I must get back to him. It was so good of you to come, Mary, and a pleasure to meet you, Percy.' She curtseyed.

'Tell me, Mary,' said Percy after she had left, 'is Adele from a wealthy family?'

'I do not know, Percy, we never talked of such things. But she lived in a grand house next to Lilian's cottage, which wasn't really a cottage, more of a mansion. I always thought the name was meant in good humour but executed in poor taste.'

Percy chewed his lip, as if an idea had formed and he couldn't quite recognise its taste. Mary knew better than to disturb the process. She scanned the room, taking in the faces of the strangers enjoying the wedding breakfast and the impromptu ditty from the chimney sweep, hired to bring good luck to the newlyweds and who must have entered the room while they were busy talking. Mary felt out of place in this season's dress, everyone else wore gowns similar to the one she'd worn for the journey up. The London ways had tainted her just as surely as the chimney sweep was stained with soot.

'I do not think Adele noticed we missed the ceremony,' Mary whispered.

'The bride and groom are only concerned with each other's presence.'

No amount of divine intervention would diffuse the evil looks that Reginald, seated next to the happy couple, was throwing in Mary's direction. Would it be better to have it out with him once and for all? But that wasn't something a lady should do and Mary did not want to spoil the wedding. It was better not to make a fuss, despite the anger bubbling inside her, letting it spill out would only arouse Percy's protective instincts and getting Percy involved might lead to all sorts of foolery — the last thing she wanted was a pistols at dawn situation; Percy had trouble enough drawing up a quill.

Speeches concluded, the hilarity of the chimney sweep tempered, it was time for the meal to be served. Percy rubbed his hands together, Mary shook her head at his boundless enthusiasm for food. His face fell when he caught sight of the food on offer, the bread and buttered rolls were perfectly agreeable but the tongue, ham and eggs and the pig's head that stared out from the centre of the table were of no use to him. Mary sighed, their shared sacrifice of sugar meant that even the tempting-looking chocolate at the end of the table and the wedding cake in the middle would be out of bounds. She piled their plates with bread rolls and buttered toast and Percy filled up the goblets.

Percy huffed. 'Do you suppose the wedding will go on much longer?'

'As long as it takes for the crowd to devour the food.'

'Do you know many people here? Except for those you knew from Dundee.'

Mary shook her head. 'No, perhaps now they are landed gentry they have invited all their workers, and those who rent their lands.'

They turned back to their rolls. Reginald had helped himself to the food, but now he sat back and resumed staring at them.

'That's it, I'm going over.' Percy threw down his napkin.

'Percy, no!' Mary pleaded. 'It will only make things worse. Let him stare at us, let him think anything he wishes to; his views on our situation have no impact upon it. Let us feel sorry for Lilian, the sweet-natured creature who has to live with a man like that.'

'I'm going to get some air.' Percy strode out. Reginald mirrored Percy's actions and Mary watched with a growing sense of unease as the two men both left the room. Lilian caught Mary's eye and her expression showed the same bewilderment as her own; what were they playing at? They had danced around each other like a pair of prize cocks. Lilian rushed over to her.

'Mary, we need to do something. Reginald thinks Percy is unnatural, that he has created an ungodly coven with you and your sister. That you are both —' she hesitated before lowering her voice — 'having relations with him.'

'Where do people get this infernal drivel?' Mary shuddered. Now wasn't the time to be going over old rumours, they had to get outside and see what was happening. The graveyard by the church was full of obstacles and if either of them should take a blow to the head and fall against a stone slab, there wasn't any coming back from that. 'Come on.'

Mary hitched up her dress and sped across the room, apologising to random people as she left, but not looking back to see the confused faces they left in their wake.

'This way.' Lilian gestured for Mary to follow her over the tall grass, trampling it down in their haste to find their quarrelling men. They could hear them before they saw them, arguing in front of the church, beside the graveyard, as Mary had feared. A strong sun glared at them as they climbed over the fence towards the church; Percy and Reginald had rolled up their sleeves, ready with loaded fists. At least they weren't pistols.

Lilian ran ahead but tripped over an object on the ground. Mary, two steps behind her, kept her gaze on the men and didn't know there was anything wrong until she heard the scream.

CHAPTER FOUR

'It's the vicar!' Lilian stammered. The body of the vicar lay at her feet.

Mary put an arm around her, stepping forward to look at the dead man; his arms were outstretched and his legs twisted tightly together, the sign of the cross. The bullet wound in his chest was still smoking. Mary cradled Lilian in her arms as she collapsed into tears.

Soon, the rest of the wedding party flocked around the body. A small, precise hole in the vicar's shirt indicated where a single bullet had killed him. Sorrow and anger quickly replaced joy as the locals threw fists and threats into the sky, yelling their disbelief at the death of a cherished member of their community.

Lilian's scream had brought Reginald and Percy to their senses, but crouched over the body, their hostility was still potent. Lilian had peeled herself out of Mary's arms at the sound of Reginald's voice and though Mary's grief was for losing the friendship she'd treasured, not the man who lay before her whom she barely knew, it was still valid.

'Who would do such a monstrous thing?' Reginald spat, his eyes wide with anger. 'We will hunt them down and kill them!'

The crowd cheered back, their matched enthusiasm proved Mary's conviction that nothing bound men together more than capital punishment. Her blood ran cold at the idea of a braying mob.

'The entire village is here, no one could have done this.' The bride stepped slowly into view, her cream-coloured gown and pale face giving her a spectral appearance. The last vestiges of colour drained from Adele's face and Mary recognised the signs and rushed over to her, collecting her in her arms before she fainted to the floor.

'Adele!' her new husband cried, his face a picture of panic; he knelt down beside Mary and took his new bride in his arms as she slowly came round.

The swooning bride quietened the crowd's anger, and the mood shifted once again.

'Everyone is here,' Adele repeated. 'We invited most of the village and the rest wish us well.' She put her hand to her head, the effort of the words had clearly been too much for her. Donald looked up towards Reginald, Mary saw the loaded glance that passed between them; it was a look that said they would not rest until the killer had been found.

'No *local* could have committed this sin.' Reginald shook his head. 'This is a Christian place and Reverend Clarke was the holiest of men, this act has been carried out by someone sinful.' He glared at Percy.

'*Me?*' Percy stepped back. 'You cannot possibly think that I have killed him? I did not know the man, what reason would I have to kill him?'

Mary hurried to her feet. She scanned the faces of the wedding guests; they had all turned towards them with the same suspicious expressions.

'You were outside with Percy too. If he's the killer, then so are you.' The words flew from Mary's mouth before she could stop them. She never could tolerate anyone badmouthing Percy, and to call him a murderer? Gossip was one thing, but this was slander. A collective intake of breath stole the air. She'd done it now, calling the respectable Reginald Ullmann a murderer. Mary bowed her head, her cheeks burning at the sudden chill in the air. 'I apologise,' she mumbled. 'I did not mean to accuse you, I merely meant to point out that the only time Percy left the wedding breakfast was when he came out here, with you.'

'I apologise also, Miss Godwin.' Mary looked up sharply. Surely that couldn't be an apology from Reginald?

'I am sorry that I have taken against you both and filled the day with hatred and scorn. Perhaps my ungodly feelings towards you both have resulted in this cruel crime against the vicar. My faith, along with Lilian, is everything to me and I cannot abide those who do not share my path.' He shrugged. 'I should be kinder to all God's creatures.'

It was the most condescending apology Mary had ever heard, but it was as good an apology as she was likely to get from him. It was typical of Reginald to get the sting in the tail and tell everyone that she and Percy were unmarried. How could he talk of cruelty when every word that left his lips was sharpened to kill?

'Thank you.' There was no point adding fuel to the fire, a man like Reginald did not give up easily. He fought to the death. 'We must put our sentiments aside and focus on the crime.'

From the corner of her eye, Mary could see Percy struggling to contain a smile. She had not meant to find herself thrust into the role of detective again, but she could see it was the only way to find peace in the situation and prove to the assembled guests that neither she, nor Percy, were the murderer.

Of all the experiences of her detecting career, interviewing a weeping bride sitting in front of a largely uneaten table of food was a new one.

'Adele, we must start with you so you can get home and begin your married life.'

'What a way to start it!' Adele sniffed into a lace handkerchief. When she rested it on her lap Mary noticed it had Adele's new initials embroidered on it: AP.

'Did you know Reverend Clarke well?'

'I've only been in Doddingley for a few months. Donald and Reginald were born here. Donald stayed, but Reginald went to Dundee. I'm sorry, I know that isn't what you are asking.' Adele burst into tears again. Mary put her hand on her arm. After an interval of sobs, Adele continued.

'I mean to say that I have only known Reverend Clarke since we have undertaken the preparations for matrimony. We had perhaps three meetings in the church.' Adele looked up. 'There was the bible reading, the conversation about matrimony and preparing the banns. That was it, I think.'

'You said that both Donald and Reginald are from Doddingley?'

'Yes, they are childhood friends. Isn't that exquisite? Still thick as thieves now. I met Donald at Reginald and Lilian's wedding. Of course, I had seen him at Charlotte's funeral.' Adele pursed her lips.

The story of Reginald and Lilian's speedy courtship raced through Mary's mind. Reginald had been married to Lilian's sister, Charlotte, but her sudden death had plunged him into a sadness that only falling in love with Lilian could remedy. It left a sour taste in Mary's mouth and a bitter hatred of Reginald Ullmann. How they had mocked his controlling ways when he'd been married to Charlotte! Now Lilian was bound by them. You would think he would be grateful for a gentle woman like Lilian, but he seemed to treat her no better than he had Charlotte, perhaps that was why he wished to marry her;

wanting another woman to control, he chose one in the marrow of one he'd previously dominated. Mary shivered at the prospect, suddenly glad of Percy's easy-going nature and kind heart. He might have his faults, but dictating her actions and who she may have as friends was not one of them.

'Do you know of anyone who would have reason to kill Reverend Clarke?'

Adele shook her head. 'No. He was a cherished member of the community, at the heart of it, from what I could see. As I say, I didn't really have much to do with him except for shaking hands after communion or pleasantries. I'm afraid I cannot really tell you much about him as a person, is that terrible?'

'No, Adele, it is not terrible, we cannot be expected to be friends with everyone we encounter and from what I know the life of a clergyman is a busy one.'

'Yes, he was always busy,' Adele agreed.

The two women sat in silence, Mary processing the information Adele had provided, Adele taking a moment to process the strange events of the day. She took a deep breath and stood up.

'Shall I ask Donald to come and see you?'

'Momentarily.' Mary paused. 'Could you ask Percy to come and see me first?'

Percy strode into the room. Mary wasn't quite sure how and when they had been separated, but the sight of him flooded her with relief. They rushed into each other's arms, grateful to find each other again, even though their separation had lasted only minutes.

'They have taken the reverend's body to Reginald's house,' Percy said.

Mary frowned. 'What have they done that for?'

'They've called the village doctor.' Percy shrugged. 'I do not know what else they think the doctor can tell them.'

'A smoking bullet means the killer was close, very close,' Mary whispered.

'What are you saying?'

'I think they mean to frame us if we cannot find an answer to this problem. What is the saying, birds of a feather flock together?'

Percy shook his head, it was something he did a lot when he couldn't find the words to articulate his feelings. Mary knew it was a sign that his mind was racing with possibilities; so long as those possibilities included a place to stay and enough money to get by, that would be sufficient. They might be here longer than either of them had expected.

'Will you stay here, behind that curtain? I want you to be here when I talk to Reginald and Donald, but I don't think I will get anything from Reginald if you are staring at him.'

'He really dislikes me, I cannot for the life of me figure out why.'

As soon as Donald sat down to speak, Mary could see nothing but sorrow towards the reverend and sorrow that Adele's wedding day had ended in such a hideous way.

'Ask me anything,' he'd said after a handshake and re-introduction.

'Adele tells me you've lived here in Doddingley all your life — what can you tell me about Reverend Clarke?'

Donald shifted in the seat, folding his arms, and pausing before he spoke.

'He was a kindly man, a good vicar, very community-minded.'

'Had he been here long?'

'Not that long, a couple of years, I think.'

'Did you know him well?'

'Reginald and I have invested heavily in the land here, that brings with it a lot of responsibilities. The reverend always helped us with families in difficulty, raising taxes, that sort of thing.'

'I did not know that was a responsibility of the clergy?' Mary scribbled it down. At moments like this, she was glad she always carried a notebook with her.

'It isn't really, but helping people is, and Reverend Clarke was very good at that, in a very dignified, subtle way, you understand.'

'Yes, of course.' Mary nodded. 'So, you cannot think of anyone who'd have reason to kill him?'

'No.' Donald bowed his head. 'He was a good man, a kind man, he will be missed.'

'This is ridiculous, we should be out there catching the killer not trapped like cattle in this room waiting for Miss Godwin to prod us.'

Mary had no intention of prodding anyone, but she supposed the analogy of detection to farming was not the worst she'd heard; besides, she had asked the wedding guests to stay until they had been questioned. It was only a matter of time until someone got impatient, and it was no surprise at all that the dissenting voice should belong to Reginald Ullmann.

'Reginald,' she replied in her sweetest voice. He turned to face her, his eyes glimmering with hatred. 'Shall we have our conversation next?' The rest of the gathered crowd fell into silence as Reginald shrugged and walked towards her, his eyes not leaving hers. Mary swallowed, gratefully remembering that

Percy was literally waiting in the wings in case Reginald proved awkward.

He sat down in the chair and folded his arms.

'You cannot seriously believe that any of us killed Reverend Clarke.'

'There is no denying his murder,' Mary replied. 'Someone must have committed that act.'

'Reverend Clarke was a cherished member of the community. There is not one person among us who has not benefitted from his charity.'

Mary sat back. She had not expected Reginald to provide such an efficient inroad to their conversation, but here it was laid out for her like a present. 'And how have you benefitted from his charity?'

'I see what you are doing, Mary Godwin.' Reginald wagged a finger at her. 'You are trying to outsmart me; do you think you can? What — because of your philosophical parents and poet lover, you think you are better than me? What gives you the right to judge me? To judge any of us?'

'I have successfully brought several criminals to justice, a whole gang of them, in fact, and this I have made known to Adele. She has asked me to investigate the reverend's death. Consider it a wedding gift to the happy couple.'

Reginald smirked. He ran his tongue over his teeth with a wolfish expression that made Mary's stomach turn.

'A wedding gift? A better gift would be your not turning up to the wedding and bringing your loose morals and *poet* with you.'

As tempted as she was to dive into a discussion of morality with a man who had courted his second wife while his first one was dying, and who had not looked further than the family home to scout out a second bride, she thought better of it. It would not surprise her to learn that Lilian had been forced to wear her sister's wedding gown. Might as well save money and save time. But this line of thought wasn't getting her answers, Mary wanted to leave Doddingley as quickly as possible, preferably with a conclusion to the crime.

'Can we return to the matter at hand? As charming as it would be to discuss love and philosophy with you — and I can see you have much to say on the subject — you have neglected to answer the question of how you, personally, have benefitted from Reverend Clarke's charity.'

Reginald fidgeted in the chair, scraping it across the floor as pushing himself further back from Mary so he could stretch his legs out and adopt a laconic, disinterested pose.

'I am a landowner with farms, tenants, workers — people who rely on my efficiency and fairness. The reverend has always been a source of help, support, and comfort. As to the specifics of how I have benefitted — I have benefitted, as all of us have, from his boundless kindness. That is all.'

'This is a religious community?' Mary continued. 'Does everyone go to church?'

'All the good people.' Reginald leant forward. 'No one in this community is capable of a crime like this, an outsider must have done it.'

'An outsider?'

Reginald nodded.

Mary could feel herself being drawn into a trap but was powerless to stop it. 'Did you see any outsiders before the reverend's body was found?'

'As a matter of fact, I did.' He straightened. 'I followed a dubious character out of the church, I did not trust him on sight.'

The curtain behind Mary rustled.

'You cannot be accusing Percy of committing this crime?'

'He was the only person to leave the wedding breakfast.' Reginald paused. 'I was watching him at the table, he seemed skittish and preoccupied, as if he couldn't settle. I thought it was nerves, but perhaps…' Reginald shrugged and allowed the rest of the sentence to float into the air.

Mary's heart raced but she would not give him the satisfaction of rising to his bait. Percy, however, was not so contained and lunged from his hiding place behind the curtain, knocking Reginald off his chair and onto the floor, where the two men grappled. Not naturally prone to anger, Percy flailed around the ground like a sea creature discovering itself on dry land. Mary watched with a mixture of bemusement and horror.

'I did not murder any vicar!' Percy's voice was shrill. He always took things so personally. Far more than she did.

'Percy!' Mary sighed. When he did not respond, she raised her voice until it became a shout. 'Percy!'

Eventually, he stopped and looked up at her.

'Please get up from the floor, Percy. Your high jinks will not help us find the killer.'

Percy and Reginald stared at each other. Restrained violence pulsed from Reginald's taut jaw but Percy's face showed nothing but hurt.

'Percy, see if you can find refreshment somewhere. My throat is parched from all this talking.'

Percy sulked out of the room, dragging his feet. Reginald sat back on the chair, dusted down his jacket, brushing Percy off with a dismissive hand. There was a cruel streak to him, just below the surface, she thought. It wouldn't take much to scratch it.

'Is that everything? Can I go now?'

Mary had learnt nothing from her conversation with him but suspected that had always been his intention; but Reginald was mistaken if he thought his bully tactics would deter her. She did not shrink away from a challenge; she rose to it and each disappointment, each knockback in life, made her more tenacious. Fearlessness was her greatest strength, she had inherited that from her mother. There were other ways to get answers, and often there was more to be gleaned by the people around the suspect than the suspect themselves. It was time to call in the next wedding guest.

While Reginald had been all arrogance and confidence, Lilian was submissive and quiet. It pained Mary to see her old friend like this, for she had always been one to light up the room with her enthusiasm and boundless joy for everything. This shell of a woman bore no resemblance to that girl of only two summers earlier, she had aged twenty years in the time and would continue this decline to its natural end too quickly if she stayed with that rogue.

'You have ignored all my letters.' Mary wanted to get straight to source of the tension between them, pulling it off like a scab and examining the wound beneath it. She already knew the reason she had been ignored, but it would be helpful to hear it from Lilian.

'I know.' Lilian lowered her head. 'Reginald does not like me to have correspondence, and he does not believe you and Percy to be the right sort of people for us.'

The right sort of people? A year ago, a comment like that would have stung, but when you are ostracised by London's entire social scene, you may as well add a few more names to the list.

'What sort of people does he suppose us to be?'

'Amoral. Ungodly. Lascivious. People who live only for pleasure and sensation.'

'Right.' Mary drew her mouth into a thin line, determined not to answer that charge. 'What else does he say about us?'

'That you are wanton for eloping with a married man while his wife was in her confinement.'

Factually, that was true, but there was so much more to the story than that. In the first flush of affection, Mary had written to Lilian about the excitement of love and the adventure of their planned elopement. She had written it with a young girl's passion, with no mind of consequence or culpability; like Lilian, Mary, too, had changed.

'I felt your loss greatly,' Mary murmured. 'We were as close as sisters in Dundee and then a sudden exodus from my life with no warning, I felt it deeply.' She still did.

Lilian sighed. 'I know, I felt it too, but Reginald is my husband and I must adhere to his commands.' She shrugged, the commands weighing heavily on her shoulders.

Mary shook her head. Society's rules were so unfair. No man should be the master of any woman. Marriage had crushed her friend like an insect.

'I would have liked to have invited you to the wedding, but...'

The reason for the lack of invitation to Lilian and Reginald's wedding did not need to be named.

'I must admit I was surprised when I heard of your marriage to Reginald.' Mary thought back to the times they had made fun of him; pulling apart each of his mannerisms and finding fault with them.

'Yes, it was quite sudden.' Lilian hesitated. 'My poor sister, Charlotte, took ill while pregnant with their child.'

Mary froze. Her grief flooded back to the surface, stinging behind her eyes and cloying at her throat.

'They lost the child, and Charlotte and Reginald were inconsolable, then poor Charlotte lost her life. We were all beyond grief.' Lilian swallowed. Mary reached out and squeezed Lilian's hand.

'I recently lost a daughter. She died two weeks after she was born.' Mary coaxed the reluctant words out. It was the first time she had said them out loud. Lilian squeezed her hand tighter.

'I am so sorry that you have known the same loss.' Lilian shook her head as if shaking off the memory. 'The only good thing to come out of that wretched, wretched time was that Reginald and I grew closer and it was decided that we should marry.'

'It was decided?'

Lilian nodded. 'My father thought it to be the most appropriate course of action.'

It wasn't hard to see what Reginald gained from the agreement, but Mary could not see how Lilian benefitted. Was there love there? Or simply convenience? How tragic that Lilian's marriage should be cast in the shadows of Charlotte, how impossible it must be for her to be her own person or learn how to be a wife on her own terms. Lilian certainly seemed more relaxed when talking about Charlotte and the earlier times they'd shared in Dundee than she was when Reginald was mentioned. Mary couldn't help but notice how her friend stiffened at the mention of his name and it saddened her. Mary thought back to her time in Dundee. Life had been simpler then, when the only monsters they faced were those they conjured in their imaginations, fed by a diet of gothic novels who they would run away from up and down the stone steps near Lilian's house. One time, Mary had fallen down the steps and felt the cold grey stone splayed underneath her outstretched hands. She'd looked at her popping veins and the stretched muscles with a new tenderness, as if seeing them for the first time. That night, her dreams had re-played the same vision, replacing the fictitious monster of their game with the one who languished in the recesses of her mind: part memory, part imagination, but all terror. The friend who had wiped away the tears from her cheeks did not fear men or monsters, but was now betrothed to both.

'Did you want to marry Reginald?'

Lilian swallowed, scrunched the handkerchief in her hands.

'There are worse husbands than Reginald, Mary. He is a good man and a fair one; he is kind to his tenants and respectable. You have only seen one side of him, there is more to him than that.'

Lilian sat straighter. Mary frowned. Was there affection there, after all? Was it possible that her singular impression of Reginald was not felt, or experienced, by those more familiar with him?

'He's a kind man. Really.' Lilian nodded, there were even the faintest traces of a smile at her lips. She was saying the right things, so why didn't Mary believe her?

The door burst open and Reginald appeared, his frame filling the door and blocking out the sunlight behind it.

'We have found the killer!'

'What?' Mary gasped.

'It was the chimney sweep.' Reginald spoke to Lilian, superiority swelling his chest. 'He was hiding out in an abandoned shed, but he ran off when we gave chase and dropped the gun.'

Mary sighed, so much for solving the crime; had that been their intention all along? Cooping her up in here like one of their chickens while they enacted their own investigation? Well, that was that then. At least they could go home. She looked at Lilian and saw her own feelings mirrored in her friend's face; disappointment that their conversation had been cut short just when they'd opened the door to their former intimacy. As soon as Reginald had barged his way in, all chances of renewing their acquaintance had stepped out.

'Where is he now?' Mary asked.

'Who?' Reginald snapped back.

'The chimney sweep. If you have caught him, would it not be opportune to hear what he has to say for himself?'

CHAPTER FIVE

'Gone, what do you mean he's gone?'

'I mean,' Reginald folded his arms and leant against the doorframe, all insouciance and arrogance, 'that he escaped.'

'You lost him?' Mary sighed. 'How are we supposed to get a confession out of him now?'

'The fact that he ran away is confession enough.'

Reginald smirked, smug in the knowledge that he'd caught the killer and Mary had not. It was no good, there was nothing Lilian could say or do to convince her he wasn't a thoroughly loathsome character.

'We've gathered a meeting in the village hall, perhaps you might come to it if you have time before you leave?' Mary could tell he was enjoying positioning her and Percy as the outsiders, pointing the finger of suspicion at him and humouring her with the pretence of actually doing something useful. If she hadn't seen Reginald get up from the table at the wedding breakfast when Percy did, Mary would have no problem in believing him to have pulled the trigger himself.

'We will come to your meeting, thank you, but we will not be leaving today. We are staying in Doddingley for several days yet so we will have plenty of time to acquaint ourselves with everyone —' Mary paused — 'and everything.'

'Oh, that is good news.' Lilian clapped her hands together, dropping them when Reginald glared at her. 'I mean, it is always good to have a holiday, is it not?'

'It is,' Mary replied.

The village hall was hot and musty, the aroma of sweat and bodies filled Mary's nostrils as soon as she opened the door. It turned her stomach and threatened to awaken her slumbering sickness. She swallowed it down and walk past rows of tuts and glances tinged with a bitterness they had not expressed before; the jovial mood of the wedding long gone. Wherever she tried to find a seat, people turned their backs to her; when they finally sat down, the woman next to her barricaded the space between them with a large lapdog who bared its teeth at Percy and Mary. Hostility did not so much hover as consume the space.

Donald commanded the room. 'We cannot let the reverend's death go unpunished. We know that the chimney sweep, Timothy Lakin, dropped the gun as he fled, what we do not know is where it has gone.' Reginald, who had arrived with Lilian, Percy and Mary, quickly took a place by Donald's side.

'He'll be headed to Overton by now if he's taken the snake path,' a voice chirped up.

'Or Dee, if he's gone in the other direction.'

'Spend all our time talking like this and he might have trekked to Ludlow!'

The chorus of voices chirped up like birds in a nest, all talking over themselves to make themselves heard. Donald put up his hand for silence.

'Quieten down everyone, please!' His voice was strained with exasperation. He rubbed at his forehead as the crowd waited for their next instruction.

'I think,' he began, 'that we need to split up into search parties, taking each of the known routes out of the village.' He looked at Reginald for confirmation, who nodded his agreement.

'He will not have got far unless he has stolen a horse — are any of the horses missing?'

'Not as far as I know,' a rosy-cheeked man replied.

'Thank you, Edward. The sun will not set for a few hours yet; we should have time enough to catch him. Edward, please can you find some oil lamps and torch lamps for each search party.' Reginald took the lead, pointing and naming people who got off their chairs and joined groups until the only people still seated were Mary and Percy.

'You two may make yourselves comfortable in your lodgings and wait for word.'

'Is there not a better use for us?' Percy replied.

'No. There is not.'

'It is not fair that we should be stuck in a tavern while the villagers are out looking for Lakin.' Percy rested his chin on his hands.

'You have a tankard of ale in front of you, Percy. I would say that there are many who would trade places with you.'

'Yes, but we should be out there, helping reprimand the criminal.'

Mary paused, taking a small sip of the warmed claret in front of her. The empty tavern where they were lodging was quiet, which brought a welcome peace to the day.

'It is not like you, Mary, to relinquish your position on a case. I expected more fire from you, more fight.'

Mary smiled but said nothing, preferring to allow her thoughts to brew before she committed them to speech. Percy, who was less comfortable with silence, shifted awkwardly in his chair.

'Mary, will you please say something? I know you have a theory about this, and I am desperate to hear it.'

'Very well, Percy.' She sighed, putting the drink down and leaning forwards. Before she spoke, she looked around to ensure that no one was listening to them. 'I think it has something to do with Reginald.'

'Lilian's husband?'

Mary nodded.

'I know you do not much care for him and having met the man, I can understand that, but what reason do you have?'

Mary shrugged her shoulders. 'Absolutely none, but I will find one.'

Too restless to retreat to their room, Mary insisted they take a walk through the village and recreate the crime scene, populating the places with as much detail as they could. First, they walked towards the church, which rested shyly in the shadow of the hill upon which the village of Doddingley sat, the scattered rice still pooled in potholes where the happy couple had trodden it into the ground. The skid marks from the abrupt halting of the carriage cut through the nearby grass, and Mary wondered if they shouldn't have just turned the carriage around and gone home. A flicker of resentment that Percy had put them in this situation resurfaced, but it was quickly replaced by her effort to remember where, exactly, they had first seen the chimney sweep.

'Was the chimney sweep outside the church as the locals were throwing the rice?' she asked Percy.

Percy thought for a moment, then shook his head.

'No, I don't think he was.'

'So he came into the wedding breakfast after the guests had sat down?'

'Yes, I think so,' Percy agreed.

'Was the vicar there, then?' Try as she might, Mary just could not picture the vicar at the wedding breakfast. The last time she remembered seeing him was outside the church. They had not been introduced, so there had been little need for pleasantries; Reginald had seen to that with his talk of them being ungodly. Her gaze had been trained on Reginald, and his preoccupation with them, that she hadn't surveyed the room with her usual scrutiny. Frustration welled up inside her.

'It is no use,' she sighed. 'I do not remember. I ignored the comings and goings of everyone except for when you went outside and were followed by Reginald. Think, Percy, think! Did you notice the vicar, or the chimney sweep, when you were outside with Reginald?'

Percy bit his lip in thought. 'No, I can't say that I did.'

'Let us go to the scene of the wedding breakfast and see if we can find anything there.'

Of all the duties Claire imagined a paid companion's role to involve, washing and styling the hair of a terrier was not one of them. Persephone had her own table for this, of course, a baroque plinth that dated from Louis IIV — so Lady Mawdsley had delighted in telling her — a plumped pink cushion, and a jewelled collar composed of gemstones Claire could neither name nor afford. Persephone had agreed to being put on the plinth easily, but had fidgeted and wriggled her way through Claire's efforts, so she knew that Lady Mawdsley's verdict on her styling would not be favourable. If she could get Persephone off the plinth in one piece, that would be victory enough for her.

'How is my darling girl?' Lady Mawdsley's saccharine tone was even more terrifying than her normal voice. 'Is she looking beautiful?'

Claire glanced at the dog, at least Persephone's eyes were visible now that she had carefully arranged the hair into two strands, thick as pony's tails on either side of her face. Beautiful wasn't the word Claire would choose.

'Good gracious, what butchery is this?' Lady Mawdsley gasped.

Claire swung around, knocking the plinth, making it tremble. Thankfully, she caught it and put it back to its correct upright position before either dog or heirloom were harmed. Persephone made an unexpected leap into Claire's arms and the weight of the dog made her stumble back again, regaining her composure with as much grace as she could muster.

'It is all the rage in Paris.' Claire bit her lip and swished the dog around quickly, hoping that the angle of Lady Mawdsley's chair might make it difficult to see the horrors that awaited at the dog's tail.

'Hmm.' Lady Mawdsley reached into her pocket for her monocle, which she attached to her left eye whilst gesturing with her right hand for the dog to be brought down lower to her. 'I suppose it does rather frame her features.' She clicked her fingers, motioning for the dog to come even closer; Persephone's fur was now practically tickling Lady Mawdsley's nose.

'Do they have a name for this style in Paris?'

'Yes,' Claire stammered, desperately scrambling through her French vocabulary in her mind until she settled on a phrase. 'They call it *Chien rideau*.'

'*Chien* ridicule more like.' Lady Mawdsley brought her hands up to the dog's hair and ruffled it so that the neat, even lines of Claire's pony tales soon dishevelled. 'There, that is better, at least it has a wave in it now, *n'est-ce pas?*'

'Very chic.' Claire nodded, putting Persephone down on the floor where the dog waited for a moment before trotting off.

'I need you to collect something for me this morning. George was telling me about his new collection — you are to collect it from the house for me. It is a most delicate operation.'

'George?' Claire asked.

'Lord Byron,' Lady Mawdsley huffed.

'You want *me* to collect something from Lord Byron?' Claire's heart raced. She had long dreamt of meeting him, but not as the paid companion of a gilded septuagenarian.

'Are you being deliberately slow-witted today?' Lady Mawdsley sighed. 'Lord Byron has asked me to host an evening of music and poetry, set to his 'Hebrew Melodies'; the poems have just been released but I am to have the version with the melodies and verse. You can play the piano?'

'Yes, a little.'

'Women are taught to downplay their talents, I'm sure yours is ample to a recitation. Can you play a sonata?' Lady Mawdsley lowered her gaze, scrutinising Claire from behind her monocle. Claire nodded. 'Then you can play these.'

Lady Mawdsley hesitated again, sucking in her cheeks. 'Actually — no offence — but it might appear a little amateur if I were to get you to play them, I don't want the neighbourhood rife with talk that I cannot afford a professional musician. No, you can learn them and play them for me today, but I'm afraid you won't be playing at the recital.'

Claire, who had no desire to play anything in front of Lord Byron, let alone the music accompanying his own poetry, breathed a sigh of relief. The bemused look that shot across Lady Mawdsley's face showed that she'd mistaken it for disappointment.

'You can come to the concert if it upsets you so much.'

Claire's expectations swelled in her chest, took bloom there. She remembered the time she'd heard a whisper that Byron would attend the anatomy lecture she had attended with Percy, Mary and James Berry; her disappointment at his failure to show had been tempered by Percy's sudden fainting fit. Perhaps if she fell into a swoon with Byron, he may be called upon to carry her to the settle. Her mind raced off in an entirely different direction until the loud coughing from Lady Mawdsley brought her back to the present.

Lady Mawdsley was staring at her with raised eyebrows.

'If you are quite finished with whatever daydream you took yourself on, you have a task to complete. Get the manuscript now, then you can work on it until high tea and play for me then. If you can play and recite the poetry, I will look most favourably on you.' Lady Mawdsley closed her eyes and nodded, as if an ancient gauntlet had been thrown down and Claire's prize would be a release from a gladiatorial prison.

Claire bowed her head. 'Which number house is Lord Byron's?'

Claire had steadied herself to knock at the door when it swung open and a crying woman burst through it, pushing past Claire and running down the street. Claire watched her go, wondering if that was Byron's new wife, latest mistress or berated servant; from the rumours she had heard, social class was no barrier to seduction. Another figure appeared in the doorway, a tired-looking woman in whose expression there wasn't even a flicker of a response to what had just happened, a sure sign that this was a regular occurrence in the Byron household.

'My name is Claire Clairmont, I'm Lady Mawdsley's companion. I'm here to collect a parcel for her from Lord Byron?'

'Parcel?' The woman sniffed. 'I don't know about no parcel. Wait there.'

She closed the door and Claire stood awkwardly in front of it, scanning the houses before moving her gaze to the green park in front of it; there, beneath a weeping willow tree, sat the woman who'd just rushed past, hunched in tears like an abandoned ragdoll. Claire watched her for a moment. No one stopped to ask if she was well or needed assistance, the only thing that seemed to offer her support or shelter was the tree which seemed to bend its branches sympathetically with each convulsion of tears.

The door opened again and a brown paper parcel was thrust into Claire's hands.

'This must be it, has it got her name on it?'

Claire looked at the parcel. There on the brown paper in Byron's dancing hand was Lady Mawdsley's name. She put her hand over the ink.

'Yes, this is for her. Thank you.'

'He asks if she can bring it back when she dines next week.'

'She's coming to dine here next week?' Claire gasped.

'Oh yes, she's a regular visitor. Good day to you.'

The door was closed again. Claire closed her eyes. It was one thing to think of breathing the same air as Byron but quite another to be getting so tantalisingly close to actually meeting him. When their paths finally crossed — as they surely must — she must refer to Percy and Mary, showcase her knowledge of Mary Wollstonecraft and all the literature and philosophy she has learnt; shared interests would be the only thing to position her as his intellectual equal, if not his social one. Now that his recent marriage had crushed all hope in that direction, the best she could hope for was acquaintance; but as she had nursed a deep and long affection for him, she feared it wouldn't take much for that to explode into love.

Claire crossed the street and walked into the park where the weeping willow branches were almost touching the head of the weeping woman. Claire stopped as she approached the tree.

'Are you in distress? Is there anything I can do to help you?' she asked.

The woman looked up, her young face a swollen red mess.

'It is nothing, I have just had a quarrel with my brother.'

'Your brother?' Claire couldn't hide the exasperation from her voice. Quarrels with her own brother Charles had never generated such high emotions. They were usually sorted by a swift punch to the arm or a sticking out of a tongue, not hysterics under a weeping willow tree. Still, if this woman was Byron's sister, then it was only natural that such dramatic tendencies might run in the family.

'I am sorry to hear that, is there anything I can do to help?' Claire sat down beside her.

'Not unless you have a talent for making unreasonable men listen to reasonable requests.' She sighed.

'I have little understanding of the minds of men and have yet to meet a reasonable one; when society allows them to be so unreasonable, it stands to reason that they would act in keeping with their role. I'm Jane.' She stretched out a hand, her old name had tripped so easily off her tongue, she hesitated for a moment, wondering if she should correct herself.

'I'm Augusta.' She stared at the hand before taking it. Claire supposed it wasn't the usual way in which women introduced themselves to each other.

'As you flew past me at Lord Byron's house, I'm presuming Lord Byron is your brother?'

'Yes.' Augusta sighed, dabbing at her face with her hands. Claire offered her a handkerchief, not realising it was one of Mary's until the embroidered 'M' stared back at her in a firm, red thread. 'Thank you.'

'That handkerchief is one of my sister Mary's, we fight like cat and dog, but I miss her.' Claire sighed, it was true.

'Is she ... dead?' Augusta hesitated.

Claire laughed. 'No, she's not dead. We have been living in each other's pockets for too long, she's moved to the country with her husband and I've stayed in London.'

All but the part of the husband was true, there was no need to say any more, even if it was Byron's sister she was sharing secrets with.

'Families.' Augusta shook her head. She had stopped crying now, and the redness was fading from her cheeks, revealing their natural porcelain hue; she looked very much like the pictures Claire had seen of Byron.

'Can I inquire what Lord Byron did to upset you so?'

'That I'd rather not say, if it's all the same. It was something and nothing about how he is treating his pregnant wife.'

'Pregnant?' Claire's jaw fell. Her hopes of romance with Byron were dwindling with every heartbeat. Then she remembered that Percy had abandoned his pregnant wife to elope with Mary; as horrible as the idea was, there was still hope.

'Yes, and he continues to be an absolute bounder.' Augusta hesitated and bit her lip. Claire, sensing that Augusta was weighing up whether to continue, grabbed her hands quickly.

'You can tell me anything. I will not tell a soul — I have no soul to tell. Apart from Lady Mawdsley, Persephone the dog, and now you, I don't know anyone else in Piccadilly Terrace.'

'You must swear not to tell a soul, Jane. Promise me.'

Augusta surveyed her with an earnest expression, clutching Claire's hands tighter and pulling her towards her. Claire nodded and swallowed down the excitement that was creeping up her throat.

'He continues to gamble, drink and take women, he will not stop.' She shrugged. 'Annabella wrote to me begging for me to come and stay and change his behaviour, but he will not change. He cannot.'

Claire fought the impulse to smile, but her hopes were reignited.

'Then all you can do is to be a friend to Lady Byron and allow me to be a friend to you.'

Augusta rushed to hug her. 'Thank you, Jane. You have given me such comfort and made me feel strong enough to go back. We must meet again, when can we meet?'

'You will find me wheeling a ball of hair in this park every morning at ten and every afternoon at four. I'm sure Persephone would love the company as much as myself.'

'Then consider us all friends.' Augusta giggled, eased herself up from the ground before giving Claire a hand and helping her up, too.

'Take care of yourself until we meet again. If you need me, I'm at Lady Mawdsley's house just over there.' Claire pointed towards the front door.

'Yes, I know where Lady Mawdsley lives, but frankly, she terrifies me, so I will meet you out here when I need your wise counsel.'

'You may have it any time.' Claire bowed.

'It has made my day meeting you, Jane.'

'Mine too.' Claire smiled. Augusta skipped off back towards the houses, her step forgetting all her previous sorrows. Claire stood for a moment, dazed by what had just happened. When she looked at the house and saw the angry shadow of Lady Mawdsley in the window, she picked up the parcel and left the weeping willow to cry alone.

CHAPTER SIX

'Any sign of Lakin?'

The villagers shook their heads as they walked past Mary and Percy to the village hall, where Reginald had called another meeting. Mary would not have known about it were it not for them overhearing it being discussed in hushed tones at the tavern, and the frost that came from Reginald's glare as he watched them take their seats confirmed they weren't welcome.

'What are you doing here? This is a local matter; it does not concern you,' he hissed.

Mary folded her arms. 'We were here when it happened, it very much concerns us and as you have been told, we have some success in solving crimes.'

'Mary has the most methodical mind, the pieces she puts together...' Percy smiled. Reginald sniggered.

'Let them stay,' Donald put his hand out to his friend. 'It won't make any difference; it isn't as if any of us can bring Reverend Clarke back.'

Reginald and Donald brought the chattering crowd to order, and Mary listened to reports of groups going in different directions finding everything from bed sheets that had flown into woodlands and given their finders a fright, to errant animals who had previously wandered off and had now been found in another field a league away. It seemed like everything lost had been found, except the chimney sweep. They had to accept the fact that Lakin had committed the crime and bolted before he could be discovered.

One by one, the locals filed out of the meeting stooped with solemnity; there was nothing so paralysing as the sensation of not being able to do anything, though all seemed to accept the explanation they'd been given. Mary remained in her seat with her arms folded and a growing sense that there was more to this story than anyone was letting on. When all but herself, Percy, Donald, Reginald and their wives remained in the room, she finally got up from her seat.

'I have one question, if I may.'

Reginald groaned. 'Yes, Miss Godwin, what is it?'

Every reminder of her title felt like a stab to the heart.

'Do you know who booked the chimney sweep?' Mary continued. 'A chimney sweep at a wedding is a symbol of luck, is it not?'

'Well, we didn't book the chimney sweep,' Donald replied. 'I presumed he just turned up — I've never been to a wedding without one.' He looked towards Reginald and Lilian, who shook their heads.

'I can't think of anyone else who would arrange one for us,' Adele spoke up. Mary remembered Adele hadn't been in Doddingley long, so her knowledge of the locals wouldn't be much better than her own.

'Lilian?' Mary asked.

Lilian stood next to her husband and blushed at the attention focusing on her. 'No, it was nothing to do with me. I helped to set up the wedding breakfast and assisted with the preparation of the food, but that was the extent of my involvement.'

'And what is known about Timothy Lakin? Is he a local man? Does he have family?'

Mary watched the faces of the couples as they digested her question. Reginald and Donald's stony expressions gave nothing away. Adele and Lilian wore expressions of people really concentrating on the question.

'A chimney sweep doesn't typically have a home and a family like a normal man,' Reginald replied. 'He follows where the work is, his home is with the rats in the slums'

'But surely he must live somewhere?'

'I'm sure he must, but I do not know where it is, do you?' Reginald spoke only to Donald, who shook his head.

'He is not one of our tenants.'

'And if he is not one of your tenants, you know nothing of his living arrangements?' Percy asked.

'I do not make it my business to socialise with chimney sweeps.' Reginald smirked. 'He is not one of our tenants, that is all I know.'

'Are there other landlords in this area?'

'There will be many, but we are the only ones in Doddingley,' Donald replied proudly. Reginald and Donald smiled at one another. Mary stiffened at the sight of their unshakable superiority.

'Just so I'm clear, you are the *only* landlords in Doddingley, you are the *only* people who rent out houses to people? Is that correct?'

Reginald sighed. 'Yes.'

'But you do not own all the houses in the village, so there must be places you do not own or know of?'

'I am sure there are, but — as you say — we do not know of them.' Reginald yawned. 'It is late, we are all tired and hungry and I am keen to get home and put this wretched day behind me. Lilian, shall we go?'

He had drifted from Lilian's side to Donald's, his two allegiances swinging like an unconscious pendulum.

'Goodnight Adele, goodnight Donald. Miss Godwin, Mr Shelley.' He kissed the first, shook the hand of the second, and gave a slight nod of the head to the third and fourth.

Outside the building, Mary watched Reginald lock the door and put the key in his pocket before the two couples walked away, chatting merrily. Mary waited until they were out of sight before turning to Percy.

'Right, Percy, we need to break into the hall.'

'Break in? Whatever for, Mary?'

'There must be a map of Doddingley, something that we can use to find Timothy Lakin's house. If nothing else, it will show us the village boundaries so we may conduct our own property searches tomorrow.'

'But Reginald said that he didn't live around here.'

Mary shook her head. 'I do not believe Reginald, he's hiding something.'

'Do you think that perhaps your own loathing of Reginald is clouding your judgement?' Percy bit his lip.

'Clouding my judgement?' She stuttered, the tempest swirling up inside her. Percy's concerned face helped to dampen it down. 'Perhaps, a little, but he would not confess to being the landlord of a wanted criminal if he was involved in the crime, would he?'

'Well, no, he wouldn't, but…' Percy paused.

'But what, Percy?'

'But I still cannot see why anyone — except for an atheist — would have a reason for the crime.'

Mary rolled her eyes; the narrow-minded views of the village were infecting Percy, and he was pointing the finger at himself, which was ridiculous. But now Mary came to think of it, Percy *had* suddenly declared a need for air at the wedding breakfast, and he always carried a pistol to unknown places in case of highwaymen. Churches, and men of the cloth, brought Percy out in a cold sweat. Was it possible that Percy, in a sudden state of frenzy, had staggered into the churchyard, been followed by the vicar, and mistaken his kindness for malice? Wouldn't Percy have then thrown away the gun for it to be found by a disbelieving chimney sweep, fawning upon it like a magpie? Could Percy have done all of this and simply blocked it from his memory? Now that the thought had entered Mary's mind, she had to conceive it was possible. And yet, there was not an ounce of malice in his body; he lived for truth and beauty, his thoughts were of nothing else. More than that, she loved him, and to believe something like that would be to admit that she did not really know him at all.

'Mary? Mary!' Percy's voice halted the hideous rattle of her thoughts. 'I've opened the door.'

The search of the village hall was useless. Whatever Mary had expected to find, she hadn't, and she came away feeling heavy with fatigue, looking forward to closing her eyes and putting the whole sorry day behind her. She felt ashamed that she had even considered Percy as the murderer — what conceivable motive could he have? But then, what plausible motive could anyone in a small, inconsequential village like Doddingley have? She was sure that it had seen more activity in that one day than it had in the rest of its history; people came to — and stayed in — a place like this because of its sleepy nature, if they'd wanted hustle and bustle, they would stay in the cities.

It was no surprise to have learned that Reginald had returned to Doddingley; the man reeked with the desire for power and Mary could see why he would relish the thought of being the biggest fish in this small pond. Donald was the type of man to easily fall in with whatever Reginald was plotting; she could picture them as small boys, Donald being encouraged to put himself in peril in order to prove himself to Reginald. Easier still to picture Reginald in miniature, flexing his power and testing the parameters of what he could get other people to do for him.

What she really needed was a breakdown of which houses, exactly, Reginald and Donald owned; she needed to have conversations with the people inside those houses away from Reginald's watchful eye and booming voice. People would be unwilling to confess their true feelings about him while he was standing in the room for fear that he might raise their rents or turn them from their homes; where power and inequality lay, there was always someone who paid the price, and it was always the person who had nothing. Having learnt from the innkeeper that Reginald's house was further up the hill from the church, known as the Big House, Mary made it her mission to call upon Lilian in the morning.

Mary slept fitfully. Her sleep brought some odd dreams that shared some of the colour of that most unexpected day. In it, she was trying to get some information but a woman kept getting in her way, shaking her head disapprovingly every time she asked a question. Eventually, her mother Mary Wollstonecraft appeared — Mary had seen her likeness — and she told the obstinate woman not to get in her daughter's way. Buoyant with a mother's belief, Mary had burst into tears that had swept through her conscious mind and dampened her pillow. It firmed her determination to find the answers to the Reverend Clarke's death. Once Percy awakened, they would go. She sat, watching him, willing him to wake, but he was so deeply entrenched in sleep that nothing she did would rise him. Instead, she took out her notebook and pencil, and scribbled down her thoughts.

'Here is what I'm thinking.' She pounced upon Percy the second he opened his eyes. Mary kissed him, picked up the notebook and paced the room. 'Reginald owns property in Doddingley, he admitted himself that most of the village are his tenants. Lilian said he is a kindly landlord, but her viewpoint might not be shared by the villagers. There has to be someone with a bad word to say about him and I will find that person.'

'You are like a dog with a bone when it comes to that man. I should worry that you are in love with him.' Percy stretched, pushing the sheets from his body, revealing his soft flesh and curves like an unveiled statue. Mary's pulse quickened at the sight, diverting her attention away from the crime and reminding her of warmth and beauty.

'How can you even joke about such things?' she said, perching herself on the edge of the bed and fighting back the sudden temptation to join him there, to bathe in the warmth of his arms. There would be time enough for that when she solved the mystery.

'There is a thin line between love and hate, Mary, a passion raised is a passion that will not be ignored.'

Mary — who was doing a fine job of ignoring her own desires — tutted and shook her head. To know herself capable of desire was enough proof of her healing for now, but to be carrying her own little memento of their last encounter was also sufficient to convince her of the urgency of concluding this business and getting home.

'I need you to find a reason to take Reginald out of his house, to get him as far away from it as possible.'

Percy frowned. 'Reginald would not even cross a bridge at my command, I don't know what you think I could say to get him out of the house.'

'Speak in his language,' Mary urged. 'His is not a poetic soul like you, he talks only of profit and loss and accountability. Talk of money and investment.'

'Money. Urgh.' Percy shuddered.

'You are thinking of buying a house in Doddingley, you find it to be a charming little village in which your creative muse stirs.'

'Go on...'

'So he will give you a tour of the properties and while you are with him, you can observe anyone who looks unfavourably on him. You are bound to notice those whose faces betray their true emotions.'

'And what will you do?'

'I will make my way into his office and see what I can find there.'

Percy and Mary stood at the entrance to the inn, surveying the village in front of them. It reminded Mary of the Parisian countryside, with its empty fields that rolled into the blue summer sky. She remembered the donkey — Napoleon — they had adopted and wondered how he was doing, hoping he was happily chewing the bounteous grass of a green field, idling away his day with his own remembrances of the strange English trio that busied his life for a brief interlude. Reginald's house dominated the distant landscape, as if monitoring the village beneath. Mary took a deep breath and walked towards the house, the Innkeeper having told Percy that he would find Reginald in his business chambers, hidden down a passageway behind the church.

The sun was harsh on Mary's back and sweat soon pinched at her neck and the base of her spine. Yesterday's golden dress had been replaced by a more sedate brown one, which she was hoping would make her blend in with the other women and make it easier to undertake her investigations without arousing suspicions. There was a chance that Reginald had not left the house yet — though Mary and Percy had been slower than intended to leave the bedchamber — and the thought of seeing him joined the constant churning sensation in her stomach. Her body had been most accommodating in keeping her secret so far, but Mary knew there were only so many times she could swallow down her nausea rather than being overwhelmed by it. The truth was, she did not want to acknowledge the pregnancy yet, for acknowledging it meant making it public, which acted as a reminder of the loss she had already encountered. It would be impossible for anyone who had known of her earlier pregnancy to separate their happiness from the sadness of the loss, it was impossible for her to navigate that ocean, so she needed to keep herself busy and a murder was nothing if not an excellent distraction.

Mary knocked at Reginald's front door and felt a tremendous rush of relief when it was opened by a housemaid rather than the owner.

'Is Mrs Ullmann available?' she asked.

'I will just see if she's taking visitors. Who may I say is calling?'

'Mary Godwin.'

The door closed and Mary wondered if it would even open again, but it did, and she was ushered into a spacious morning room the colour of daffodils. Lilian appeared as fragile as the white lace gown she was wearing.

'This is a pleasant surprise, Mary.' Lilian smiled. 'I did not know if you would have already departed for London.'

'We have decided to stay for a couple of days. Doddingley is such a charming place.'

Lilian nodded. 'That is good to hear, will you take tea?'

'I will. Thank you.'

'If you'll just excuse me for a moment, I will see to it.'

Mary stiffened at the formality of Lilian's tone; even the gentle nudges back towards their former friendliness had gone. Lilian was talking to her with the clipped politeness of a stranger, given to unexpected morning callers. Mary used Lilian's brief absence to search through the drawers of the desk, finding nothing but parchment, quills, and a prayer book. This was clearly Lilian's room. What she needed was to find Reginald's office.

When Lilian returned with the maid and the tea, Mary was back in position, her dress neatly smoothed out and her unruffled features giving no hint of the madness of the preceding minutes. Once the tea had been poured and the maid had left the room, Mary got straight to the point.

'I need your help, Lilian.'

'What can I do for you?'

'I need a map of Doddingley, and I need you to tell me who lives where and which of the houses Reginald owns.'

'Reginald and Donald, you mean, they are business partners? Reginald does not have enough money of his own to buy houses, not even with my marriage portion.'

'Your marriage portion?'

'Well, yes, of course I had a marriage portion and a small annual sum. It is the way weddings work, Mary, we cannot all rely on our natural charms and beauty to find us a match.'

Mary's stomach tightened at the reminder of her status. She could not imagine her father proffering so much as a quill if Mary and Percy were to marry; she had fallen so far into the abyss that no amount of societal rope could pull her out of it.

'We must be quick in this, Lilian, if you will help me, you must do it now.'

'You cannot believe that Reginald has something to do with the reverend's death?'

'I believe there is more to it than we think, and I need to find the truth.'

'And having a map of Doddingley and finding out the names of Reginald's tenants will help you do that?'

'I need to talk to as many people as I can, Lilian and those closer in social stature to Lakin may have more information about him.'

'Or no further information whatsoever. Perhaps the crime is exactly as it seemed, Mary.' Lilian hesitated.

Mary detected a hint of sarcasm in her tone, or was it something harder — mistrust? Whatever it was, it was soon deflected when Lilian shrugged her shoulders and smiled.

'Very well. I will draw you a map and give you the name of each of the occupants.'

CHAPTER SEVEN

The shocked expression that swept across Reginald Ullmann's face as he opened the door to Percy Shelley told his visitor that the visit was not welcome. Nevertheless, Percy stepped forward, which gave Reginald no choice than to open the door wider and allow him into the building. Percy strode forward, stopping to admire the rich red decoration and shimmering gold touches which seemed a little ornate for a place of work, but Percy was too polite to make such a claim.

'I find myself quite enamoured of your village,' Percy began. Reginald, who was walking ahead of him, turned around with a sly smile, which showed his disbelief in Percy's claim. Percy smiled back, hoping that his face communicated something like sincerity, though there was some element of truth to his words — he found the village charming even if some of its inhabitants had been less than welcoming. 'I am thinking of buying a property here and I thought you and Donald would be the best people to ask, you seem to have your finger on the pulse of everything.'

'That's very interesting.' Reginald stroked his chin.

'I know you're a busy man,' Percy continued. 'Could you spare some time to show me around?'

'There aren't many houses to choose from.' Reginald sat at his desk, inviting Percy to sit in the opposite chair. 'Ours is a very rural community and houses of the style that you are used to are few.'

'I have money,' Percy added quickly. 'My grandfather recently gave me a handsome advancement on my allowance.'

Reginald sat up straighter, the talk of money clearly making the conversation more attractive to him. Mary was right, this was certainly the way to get Reginald Ullmann's attention. Percy wondered how far Reginald would go in the pursuit of it.

Minutes later, they closed the door behind them, walking into the bright sunny day. The sunshine illuminated the village's best features, making the church's stained-glass windows glow in the distance like a pair of brilliant eyes, the gravestones blanched by the sunlight turning the stone maidens and monuments into fine marble statues. The landscape was dotted with livestock and farm buildings were scattered here and there like pieces on a chessboard. People lived out gentle lives within them, taking their cues from the seasons, reading its rhythms and dictates, allowing life to come and go as it will. Percy had long sought the tranquillity of the countryside — it had been part of the reason for the move to Windsor. The need to escape from a gang of grave-robbers who might be out for revenge was another one. Something about Doddingley reminded him of Cwm Elan, but the memory of his time in the Welsh valley with Harriet cast a dark shadow over his thoughts. The distant crack of a gunshot in the fields reminded him of his own attack and soon the loud beat of his elevated pulse drowned out all of Reginald's conversation.

'Well?' Reginald asked.

Percy did not want to confess that he had not paid attention, so he simply smiled and nodded in agreement. It turned out that what he had agreed to was a tour of all Reginald's properties; a showcase — Reginald's opportunity to show off exactly what he owned and how much power and position he had in the village. He had tumbled straight into Percy's trap. All he had to do was observe the interactions between

Reginald and his tenants and make a mental note of any relationship that seemed strained. Then — if Mary had secured some sort of map from Lilian — compare this information with hers and a fuller picture of Reginald's position in the village may be garnered; though Percy was still at a loss to what exactly Mary was planning on doing with the information.

'Have you ever thought of becoming a landlord yourself?'

'Me?' Percy laughed. 'No, I have trouble enough with my own finances, I would hate to be entrusted with others — rents and rates and dealing with difficult tenants, no that is not a job for me.'

'I dare say that I would not enjoy the life of a poet,' Reginald retorted. 'Though I imagine it to be infinitely eased by an allowance.'

Percy's cheeks flushed, how dare Reginald be so condescending? There was not an ounce of poetic feeling in his entire body, that much was clear merely from looking at him. Reginald possessed the same obsession with wealth and appearances as his father and grandfather. Percy had never truly fitted in with the family and had always felt as though he were a bitter disappointment to them both.

'Personal feelings aside,' Percy strained to keep his voice level, 'shall we press on with our tour? I don't want to keep you from your business.'

Reginald nodded, holding out his hand to indicate that Percy should proceed. They walked towards a smallholding near to the church, half-hidden and quiet on the landscape. This cottage gave no clue as to the nature of its inhabitants.

'Perhaps this might be a suitable house?' Reginald said. 'It is no London townhouse, but it is charming, comfortable and private.' Percy could not deny that it looked charming and private from the outside, but he would only know if it were comfortable by venturing inside it.

Reginald knocked at the door. Percy frowned, it sounded like there was a chicken squawking behind it. He was even more confused when an elderly woman answered the door.

'Mrs Harris.' Reginald spoke firmly.

'Yes?' the old lady answered, pulling her shawl closer around her shoulders. 'Who are you?'

'Your landlord, Reginald Ullmann.'

'What do you want? We're not behind with our rent, so you'll not be sending your men to us.'

Reginald had men to collect his rents? That was useful to know. Though it had to be said that Reginald was not the type of man to shy away from a confrontation, if Percy's own experiences were anything to go by.

'No, Mrs Harris, nothing like that, but you may remember our previous discussions on the sale of the property. Mr Shelley here would like to look around it.'

'I'm not up the River Tick yet, Mr Shelley, don't be marking me out as one who doesn't pay her way.'

'Is Mr Harris at home?' Percy asked.

'Mr Harris?' she spat. 'He drank himself into the grave seven years hence — you'll find him at the churchyard if you wish to make his acquaintance.'

'No, no, I was just … making conversation.'

'If you're coming in, you'd better be quick about it, otherwise the chickens will get anxious.'

The squawking resumed and before long, Percy and Reginald were surrounded by dozens of chickens pecking them into a circle, before a sharp whistle from Mrs Harris made them retreat to wherever they had come from.

'Sorry about that, they get very protective.'

The chickens weren't the only animals in the house, rabbits and cats seemed to occupy every surface. The stench of animals and the hair that stuck to Mrs Harris's clothes and every other piece of fabric in the cottage made Percy's eyes water and his skin itch; even if he was a genuine buyer, this was an effectively subtle way to put a purchaser off the property.

When they closed the door behind them, Percy gulped at the fresh air, grateful for the sudden wind that cleared his sinuses and his streaming eyes. Reginald stormed on ahead, muttering to himself about Mrs Harris and her odd ways. The second house on their trail was smaller than the first but surrounded by more farmland. Its inhabitants were soon revealed to be Mr and Mrs Evanson and they did not look happy to be opening the door to Reginald Ullmann; in fact, Mr Evanson picked up a pitchfork to get him off the property, which was not the done thing when dealing with a landlord. Reginald squirmed under this spotlight, clearly this was a household that he left to his 'men'.

The third cottage they visited was hidden on a circular track that spiralled around the back of the church in the shape of a question mark. Reginald had long since discarded terms like 'charming' or 'comfortable.' As they walked towards the house, a bucket of slop was thrown in their direction, lightly splashing Percy but soaking Reginald. He tried hard to stifle a laugh as Reginald shook the filthy water off himself, muttering curses as he spat out mouthfuls of liquid.

'I'm sorry, Mr Ullmann, I didn't see you there,' an elderly man stuttered. He locked eyes with Percy, and Percy recognised the glimmer in his eyes that signified his true intention of throwing the slop. Reginald was too preoccupied with himself to notice the bond of loathing that bound Percy and this stranger together.

'This is Mr Shelley, he was interested in buying a property in the village, but no doubt your antics have dispelled him of those notions.'

'Oh, I am sorry, Mr Shelley, don't let the stupidity of an old man put you off Doddingley. It's a lovely place with *some* lovely people.'

'Come along, Mr Shelley, there are other places.'

Percy made a mental note that two of the three houses they had visited contained people with a visible dislike of Reginald; if the current statistics were met out over the rest of the houses, that would mean that over half of his tenants did not like him. When Reginald stopped to take off his jacket and flap it in the wind to rid it of the liquid that saturated it, Percy made a note of the inhabitants and the location of the houses so that he and Mary could come back without Reginald and ask them what they really felt about him — above the sentiments reflected in their actions.

A wet jacket seemed to dampen Reginald's enthusiasm for the tour, and it was swiftly concluded with only the addition of another two houses. Having undertaken the tour of the village, Percy was reluctant to agree with Reginald's earlier assertion that there weren't any properties suitable for him and Mary. Walking back towards the church — and Reginald's business property by the side of it — Reginald pointed out the hut that housed the chimney sweep, Thomas Lakin. A small, shabby affair made of wooden wattles, the panels had warped, and weevils had eaten a way through the structure, revealing thin strips of light from inside it. Percy frowned.

'I thought you said Lakin did not have a house in Doddingley?'

'I said he did not rent a house from Donald and I,' Reginald countered. 'I would not rent that to a pig.'

'Could we take look at it?' Percy asked.

Reginald frowned. 'Why on earth would you want to look in here? A man of your means has no business with low lodgings like this.'

Percy did not want to admit that it might offer some clue that would help make sense of why the chimney sweep had shot the vicar and why he had absconded so quickly afterwards. Instead, he shrugged and said simply, 'Curiosity, I suppose.'

Reluctantly, Reginald tried the door. 'Unlocked. Nothing of value inside.' Reginald pushed the door, but it would not fully give.

'That's strange,' he said.

'Let me try.'

Percy stepped forward, pressing his shoulder to the door with all his might. Eventually, the wood cracked and the door swung open, revealing the hanging body of Thomas Lakin inside.

The chimney sweep hung from the rafters from a tightly bound sheet around his neck. His face still wore the soot mask of the wedding and the ragged clothes that uniformed his role. Percy gaped. It was his second dead body this week, something unheard of in a town like Doddingley.

Reginald quickly took charge, instructing Percy to hold the body while he untied the sheet and, for a moment, the corpse of Thomas Lakin fell into Percy's arms like an autumn leaf falling from a winter tree. Once they'd got the body down, Reginald hoisted it over his shoulders, lifting it as if it were weightless.

'I must get him to Dr Snelling for confirmation of the time of death.'

'Would it not be better to bring the doctor here, so he may see the circumstances of it all?'

'We are both witness to the circumstances of it all, there will be no doubt on that matter.'

'I shall come with you then.'

'No.' Reginald stopped, his motion causing the chimney sweep's arm to flay out unexpectedly, almost slapping Percy in the face. Percy dodged out of the way. 'There is no need for that. Do you know of my house? It is the one they call the Big House. Donald's house is next door. Find Donald and let him know what has happened. We must raise a meeting with the community. He will arrange that.'

Percy nodded, unable to take his eyes from the dead man, taking in all the details he could — how the hands were still floppy and not set to stone, how the skin appeared blue where the soot had wiped clean. If Reginald were not watching him so intently, he would have written all these details down. Instead, he nodded agreement and set out towards the Big House, only stopping to watch Reginald carry the body to the doctor's.

Mary was just leaving Lilian's house when she spied Percy rushing towards it, breathless and wide-eyed.

'Percy, what is it?'

'We have found him, the chimney sweep — he is dead!'

Lilian ushered him into the house and saw to it that tea quickly followed. Although abstaining from sugar, Percy nodded at the offer, and the relief that spread across his face as he drank the sweet liquid proved that he had needed it to revive him. *It must have been a terrible shock to find another dead body*, Mary thought. How quickly this small place was disposing of its residents, and what a terrible start to Donald and Adele's honeymoon period.

Percy had recounted the details of the grisly discovery, detailing the houses he and Reginald had visited beforehand, which Mary made a mental note of, that, she supposed, was the end of the mystery, no need to talk to the locals to get a picture of the suspected criminal; he had killed himself because of the weight of the guilt, there was nothing more to uncover. All that remained was the chimney sweep's motive for the crime, and the dead take their secrets with them.

'I suppose someone should tell Donald and Adele.' Lilian spoke slowly, her voice tremulous. It was clearly not an undertaking she wished to take alone.

'Reginald wants Donald to call a meeting for the villagers, to tell them the news and put the matter to rest,' Percy confirmed.

'If you are already going, I do not suppose that I am needed?' Lilian's tone was hopeful. Lilian seemed so accomplished in that understated, respectable way of a middle-class wife, but her heart beat with the young girl's insecurities. Mary reached out to her, gently placing a hand on top of hers.

'You need not go if it is too much for you. Being strangers here, Percy and I have the necessary detachment for the delivery of bad news.'

'It is just too much death.' Lilian reached for her handkerchief. Poor Lilian, few had known as much loss as she — it was no surprise that the additional losses of the last few days had brought the other griefs to the surface. 'What a start to married life!'

Mary held Lilian as she sobbed. If this was what a wedding and a marriage would bring, she found herself suddenly very pleased to be single.

Lilian saw them off with eyes still wet with tears, despite her best efforts to curtail them. She waved and smiled weakly, but Mary knew she would feel an instant sense of relief once safely back behind her door. For Mary and Percy, they were the deliverers of bad news, and both took a deep breath as they knocked on the door to Donald's house. The man who opened it instructed them to wait inside, informing them that both master and mistress of the house were at home. Though the house was smaller than Reginald's, the interior decoration was every bit as opulent, the colour scheme neatly matching that of Donald's friend. Yellows and regal reds were the colours of the season and the mock-classical look favoured in Reginald's was also on show here; Reginald's influence ran deep.

Moments later, Donald and Adele entered the room. Percy blurted out the news with no attempt to cushion it, and both Donald and Adele gasped and put their hands to their mouths.

'No!' Adele spoke first. 'Dead? By his own hand?'

Percy nodded. 'Hanging from the rafters '

Mary watched as Donald's expression changed from shock into something more forceful, anger perhaps. He worked his jaw with loud, repetitious motions.

'Donald?' his wife asked. 'Are you well?'

He appeared to be in some sort of a trance. When he finally opened his mouth, the words came out in a slow mumble.

'Coward's way out,' he said. 'Would not take his punishment like a man. Coward's way out. White liver.'

Adele turned to Mary. 'He's in shock,' she whispered. 'Help me get him to the settle.'

Together they gently guided Donald to the settle where he sat, oblivious to those around him. Mary and Percy exchanged a look of confusion that was quickly noticed by Adele.

'He gets like this sometimes. It is nothing to fear. He will be all right soon.'

'What is it?' Percy whispered, staring at Donald as if watching an exhibit at the Royal Menagerie.

'I don't know,' Adele whispered back. 'Dr Snelling couldn't give me a name for it. It is his way of processing trauma, apparently. You just watch, he will snap out of it in a moment.'

Sure enough, Donald shook his head and returned to his former senses. Mary frowned, fainting fits and such were quite unusual occurrences in men, she thought. The only other one she had seen was when Percy fainted during the autopsy in London. Was it real? Or some kind of trick to turn talk away from the murder? Something about the speed with which he snapped in and out of his trance-like state smacked of insincerity. But she knew little of such things. She made a mental note to ask James Berry what he knew of such occurrences.

'Reginald wants to call a meeting of the villagers to tell them what has happened,' Percy continued.

Donald nodded. 'Will you accompany me? This is not the work for ladies.'

Mary bit her lip to contain her mirth, talking to her old friend was infinitely more welcome a prospect than going from house to house and calling a meeting.

'May I have a quick word with Percy before you go?' Mary asked, ushering Percy out of the room. 'He will meet you outside, Donald. Adele, I will be back in a moment.'

'I will arrange for more tea.'

'Percy, what is your feeling about this?' Mary asked once she and Percy were outside, her face flushed with excitement.

'My feeling about what, dear?'

'The chimney sweep coming back to take his own life the day after he's killed Reverend Clarke. Does that seem normal to you?'

'I have no conception of what is normal to a murderer, Mary, as I have no experience of being one. Have you?'

'No, of course not. But does it not strike you as highly convenient?'

Percy frowned. 'What?'

'That the body of the chimney sweep is discovered as soon as we started asking questions? I know we asked questions on the day of the wedding, but we were rather thwarted in our efforts then.' Mary stopped, her eyes widening as a thought suddenly struck her. 'Wait! We were halted in our efforts by Reginald, and who found the body today? Reginald! Does it not seem to you like an effort to appease us? To answer those questions we are — *were* endeavouring to answer?'

'It seems like a tremendous amount of effort, Mary.' Percy sighed. 'Is it not possible that the explanation that presents itself is, in fact, what actually happened? That for some reason, the chimney sweep shot the vicar and then, knowing he was being pursued and would go to the gallows, took his own life?'

Mary folded her arms. 'It still does not answer why the chimney sweep wanted to kill the vicar, what motive he may have.'

'Mary, my love, I think you need to accept that we may never discover what the motive was.'

Mary frowned. Percy might believe they may never discover the truth, but she did not.

CHAPTER EIGHT

The hall was crowded and noisy, the local community whipped into a state of frenzy by the unwelcome discovery of yet another dead body. The voices that floated through the air confirmed Donald's feeling that Lakin had taken the coward's way out rather than face the due process of law that would have ultimately had the same result.

Mary and Percy took their seats as Reginald and Donald marched to the front of the hall and the meeting was brought to order. Percy sat with the fresh knowledge of many present nursed a private dislike or distrust of Reginald, while Mary could not shake the feeling that someone here wanted everyone to believe the case was firmly closed in order to draw suspicion away from himself.

'Thank you for coming,' Reginald began. 'We called this meeting to confirm the capture of Thomas Lakin — and his death.'

The crowd erupted into cheers; Mary put her hand to her chest as the surprise overwhelmed her. Once the crowd settled down again, Reginald continued.

'His death brings the matter of the death of Reverend Clarke to a close. The coroner is satisfied with the cause of death and has released the body for burial. Reverend Clarke's funeral will take place on Friday. His body will be dressed by Mrs Harris. Come and pay your last respects to this fine man and help our community move on from the tragedy of this whole sorry affair.' Reginald's voice cracked and he turned his face away from the crowd as emotion overwhelmed him. Donald took over.

'This week has been unlike any other I have known in Doddingley; I have never experienced such happiness and such sadness at the same time. We must strive to get back to the community we were before Lakin's foul deed devastated us.'

Murmurs and the stamping of feet confirmed the crowd felt the same way. Percy looked at Mary and shrugged, as if to say, 'Well, that's that then.' The villagers may be able to accept the conclusion of events, but she could not, and the sensation that something was not quite right pulsed in her veins, matching the stamping of the crowd, and getting louder and louder.

Reginald turned back to face the people, his features resuming their customary scowl. He seemed energised by the noise of the crowd; he breathed in deeply, pushed out his chest and roared like a lion. The audience applauded and looked at him with something Mary could only describe as devotion. What a hold he had over them, how easily his own mood dictated theirs, what power that was. Donald, by his side, looked bemused by his friend's antics, frowning at Reginald, and scanning his face as if trying to find the meaning of his action; before he too roared. The audience leapt to their feet, leaving Mary and Percy at the end of their row, seated outsiders trying desperately to understand what they were watching.

Shortly afterwards the crowd dispersed. Mary and Percy rushed out before everyone else, hiding behind a tree in order to watch them leave. All wore contented expressions, as if they had been cleansed of some great demon that had possessed them all.

'What was that all about?' Percy whispered.

'I do not know,' Mary replied. 'Reginald seemed to bewitch them all, it felt like they would have darted off like a pack of hounds in pursuit of an animal if he'd asked them to.'

'He certainly seems to have a lot of power,' Percy agreed.

'But he and Lilian have only been back in Doddingley for a year, they were in Scotland before that. How does someone get so much power in a year?'

'I will tell you how, Mary — money.'

Mary awoke early the next morning, the dawn chorus melodiously bringing her to her senses while the sun streamed through the window, bringing a warmth to her face. Percy slumbered beside her, his arm outstretched. She planted a delicate kiss on his cheek, which made him smile in his sleep and turn on to his other side. Gently, she slid out of the bed and padded across the room, picking up her notebook and pencil. She tapped the pencil against her lip as she tried to make sense of everything that had happened. The villagers seemed satisfied that Thomas Lakin had killed Reverend Clarke. Why would a local man choose a public event like a wedding, to which it seemed the entire village had turned out, to kill a man? Would it not have been easier to kill him when the eyes of the village were turned away? But then, if they had all been at the wedding breakfast, what better opportunity to lure the vicar outside for a private chat and shoot him?

From what Mary knew of weddings — and other than her father's wedding to Mary Jane, she knew very little — it was unusual to have a wedding breakfast on the scale that Donald and Adele had undertaken; William Godwin's had been a modest affair with a small wedding breakfast for the happy couple and their children. Donald and Adele's grand breakfast was either a sign of the community's affection for them or perhaps Donald's compensation for Adele's lack of family; Mary could believe that he would want Adele to feel cherished and special on their wedding day. Donald seemed to be in

Reginald's shadow, the mediator of Reginald's moods, the one who would soften harsh blows thrown down by Reginald and offer soothing words and comfort to those in trouble. He had a more serene air than Reginald, who always seemed — to Mary — as if trying to prove himself with everything he said or did.

Wedding breakfast aside, that still did not offer a motive for Lakin's behaviour. From what Percy had said, Lakin's lodgings had been modest, primal even, so an occurrence of debt or disfavour seemed unlikely; if there could be no question of him being in financial trouble, what reason would he have for killing Reverend Clarke? Unless his crime was of the spiritual kind, and he was afraid his sins were about to be revealed. Was Lakin afraid that the good reverend was about to make too merry and become loose-lipped? Mary regretted not having spoken to the vicar more outside the church, she may have learned something more of his character; but then, she had not expected a murder to follow on from a wedding so swiftly.

'How long have you been awake?' Percy murmured from the bed.

'The sunlight woke me; it is so bright today it is hard to tell the time. I have been trying to make sense of the deaths. Does it not seem odd that Lakin should come back to the village and take his own life days after running away?'

'Everything about this village seems odd.' Percy sat up in the bed. 'The sooner we are away from it, the better. The case is closed, and I am keen to get back to civilisation.'

'We will stay for the funeral and then we can leave. Arrange the carriage for Friday afternoon and we shall be home for Sunday.'

'All this religion is bringing me out in hives.' Percy scratched his neck and Mary laughed at him.

*

'Remind me what we are trying to achieve?' Percy asked as they walked from the inn to the church.

'I want to talk to those people who expressed a dislike for Reginald.' Mary held the map Lilian had made for her firmly in one hand, her pencil in the other.

'Mrs Harris was very rude to him and the man from this house doused him with dirty water.' Percy pointed to a house on the map. 'I never learnt his name, he was an elderly man who blamed his poor eyesight for it, but he knew exactly what he was doing.'

'I have a theory — and it is only a theory, mind — that Reverend Clarke must have known something about Lakin and that is the reason for his murder.'

'But how does that link with Reginald?'

'I don't know.' Mary sighed. 'Perhaps the secret involves Reginald, too?'

'But if it does, then we are unlikely to learn it from other people.'

'I know.' Mary shrugged. 'So far, no one has had a bad word to say about Reginald, everyone talks of him as a fair man, but that is not the man I see. I think there is more to him, I really do.'

Percy put an arm around her shoulders as they walked. 'Will you not entertain the possibility, Mary, that your dislike of the man is clouding your judgement? He is a peacock and a prig, but a murderer? No, I do not think so.'

'You are probably right, but I need to know more about him. Here we are.'

Mrs Harris's chickens clucked excitedly outside the door before making their way towards Mary and Percy, who froze to

105

the spot. The chickens surrounded them, their beaks darting closer to the fabric of Mary's dress and Percy's trousers.

'Who's disturbing my chickens?'

'Mrs Harris?' Mary asked. 'My name is Mary Godwin and this is Percy Shelley, we are friends of Lilian Ullmann. I've come to talk to you about Reginald Ullmann, if you can spare us a moment of your time?'

Mrs Harris whistled, and the chickens moved away from Mary and through the open door Mrs Harris gestured towards. Once the chickens had entered the house, Mary and Percy followed.

'This isn't one of your grand houses, so I won't be offering tea.' Mrs Harris sniffed, gesturing for them to go through to the kitchen, where she sat on a stool in front of a stack of potatoes. 'You don't mind if I carry on my chores while we talk?' She picked up her knife and started scraping away at the potato skin before Mary could answer.

'Percy visited your house recently, with Reginald Ullmann.'

'That's right. Looking to buy a property, aren't you? I wouldn't bother, Ullmann's stolen them all.'

'Stolen?' Mary's ears pricked up. 'What makes you say that?'

'He's only been here a year and they've bought up all the houses, there's not a one here that him and Donald don't own. That house he's in, the Big House, that was my former home.'

'You used to live there?'

'Don't seem likely now, does it? It was in my family for years until my late husband got behind with his taxes and we had it taken off us.'

'Taken off you?' Percy repeated.

'You two are like a pair of parrots.' Mrs Harris pointed the knife at them. 'Are you simple in the noggin' or something?'

'Reginald purchased the house because of your husband's debts?'

'That's about the size of it.' Mrs Harris sniffed again. 'He bought me this one instead, not a patch on the old one.'

When she'd opened the door, Mary had presumed Mrs Harris to have lived a lifetime in the same vein. She'd seen only the worn woollen cap on her head, the shabby clothes that were almost as wrinkled as her skin. There was no indication of her ever belonging to a different social class. Mary was ashamed that she'd been so judgemental, the twist in her stomach soon reminded her of the previous winter in which money had been so scarce that they'd survived on water and biscuits — she of all people should know how quickly financial situations could change.

'He took over the sale, used the money to pay off my husband's debts, and we moved in here.' Mrs Harris picked up another potato and started peeling. 'I buried him six weeks later.'

Mary and Percy bowed their heads, giving Mrs Harris a moment to reflect on her grief. Even the chickens fell silent.

'So, you see, that is why I cannot tolerate the man. He killed my husband as surely as if he'd taken a gun and shot him in the heart.'

It was a similar story at the old man's cottage — rents raised to prices their tenants could not afford, houses repossessed and families forced into smaller, less comfortable houses. This picture of Reginald did not match the smooth public persona that Mary had witnessed in action at the village hall. She was delighted that her suspicions of Reginald's character had been proved right.

'I still think you are letting your own feelings guide you, rather than considering the facts,' Percy cautioned as they took a stroll through the woodlands. 'If Reginald is as dangerous as you think he is, you would be better to stop stirring the hornet's nest.'

'He does not scare me,' Mary huffed. 'If we can survive a murderous husband and a gang of resurrectionists, we have nothing to fear from a country dandy.'

'That's as may be, but London has more hiding places — this is a small village and murders happen quickly and are silenced with the same speed.'

'So, you think they have been silenced?' Mary raised her eyebrows. Percy nodded, a small smile creeping to his lips.

'I confess that my curiosity is not as easily satiated as that of the locals, but we do not live here, Mary. We cannot stay here forever and nor would I want to. Let them sort out their own problems. Let us return to our own home and our own lives and leave them to it.'

'I know you are right.' Mary sighed. 'There is a part of me that wants to prove to Lilian that Reginald is unworthy of her, but she knows what he is like, and she has accepted it. It is I who cannot accept the situation.' Mary bit her lip. 'Seeing Adele and Lilian just reminded me of how it was to have friends, good friends. I miss them.' A tear ran down Mary's cheek, the delicate sadness of an unacknowledged regret surprising her.

Percy hugged her. 'It is hard when people turn you out of their lives for no good reason; but at least with Lilian, you know it is Reginald who has forced the separation, not Lilian. Your friendship will endure and renew, have a little patience, my love. All will be well again.' Percy kissed her tenderly on the head. Mary's heart swelled with love for him, and she cupped his face and kissed him hard on the mouth. Astonishment and delight danced across his features and they gazed at each other as the sun smiled down on them.

'That is enough investigating for one day,' Mary said, taking his hand. 'Let us go back to our room.'

CHAPTER NINE

A grey sky cloaked the village in solemnity the morning of the funeral. Church bells rang out in slow, repetitive chimes that mimicked the movement of the coffin. Reginald, Donald, and the other young men from the village took the coffin on their shoulders and shuffled towards the church. A man, his attire as black as a crow, carried ostrich feathers in front of the coffin. All heads were bowed, the entire village turning out for the second ceremony in a week. Mary and Percy took their place among the congregation, sitting at the back of the church, putting a respectable distance between themselves and the mourners. Lilian and Adele were at the front, their backs straight, but when they turned back, Mary saw their expressions were as crumpled as their handkerchiefs.

The new vicar walked briskly over to the lectern and all thoughts were drowned out by a stentorian voice that boomed into the church's vacuous ceiling, shaking the candelabra. Mary surveyed the congregation: all faces were waxy with grief, all mouths were downturned. Even when knelt in prayer, she did not fully close her eyes, Percy's warning that they were in danger hummed in her head as the service continued. They presented a threat to the community, though why Mary couldn't quite tell. Whatever the reason, it was enough to make them pack their belongings and call the carriage to collect them. Mary knew Percy felt a sense of relief at getting out of Doddingley, but she knew that as soon as there was a geographical gap between herself and Lilian that their emotional distance would resume.

All sermons concluded, all dedications done, the service ended, and Mary held back, allowing the other mourners to leave the church before they did. Adele and Lilian caught her eye as they walked past, smiling weakly as they turned out of the church. When it was their turn to leave, Mary hesitated, her mind turning to detection, wondering if there might be some way of accessing church records of payments and transactions; the stern face of Christ glared out from the stained-glass window, his hand raised in sorrow. Mary bowed her head and made her way out of the church.

'Mary, the carriage is ready.' Percy put his hand on her arm. She had been so wrapped up in her thoughts that she hadn't noticed he'd left her side or the advancement of time to the hour of their scheduled departure, so much for being observant.

'So soon?' The words caught in her throat. She was not ready to say goodbye to those she'd only recently got back in her life. 'Have I time to say goodbye to Adele and Lilian?'

'They are going for the interment of the body.' Percy nodded towards the mourners, moving up the incline to the top of the graveyard where the vicar's gown blew in the breeze like a ship's sail.

'I had best not disturb them.' Mary sighed; her body heavy with regret. Despite all the sorrow they had witnessed in Duddingley, it had not been *her* sorrow and the reprieve from the house in Windsor and all its memories of their beloved child Clara had been more welcome than she had realised.

'Let us go.' She took Percy's hand and they made their way in the opposite direction, where the outline of the carriage cast a black shadow on the green landscape.

'I do hope we have a different driver,' Mary whispered, relieved to discover that not only did they have a different driver, but this carriage had windows. At least it would be more comfortable in this heat. Percy helped her step into the carriage.

Percy took a seat beside her, holding her hand as she gazed out of the window, taking a last look at Doddingley. Lilian and Reginald were standing side by side, stiff as statues but looking every inch a couple sure of their place in this world. Adele and Donald stood next to them, Donald to the right of Reginald, where he had always been. Reginald was clearly a man of great loyalty and feeling, but where Mary was concerned, he did not seem to concern himself with the consequences of forbidding their friendship. It was clear to Mary from the short amount of time she'd spent alone with Lilian that she was not so much changed, there was nothing in their own natures that should prevent their friendship, only the dictates of Reginald and a society that enabled men to have all the power and women to be nothing more than another possession. It was wrong, all wrong, and though her own mother had done much to draw attention to society's inequalities, her life had ended before she'd seen the reform she craved. Nothing had changed and Mary doubted that anything would — not in her lifetime, anyway.

'Goodbye Doddingley.' She waved through the open window, though she knew no one would wave back.

'Off we go.' Percy tapped the side of the carriage and the horses set off with a jolt, tipping Mary and Percy back against the seat. Composing themselves, Mary leant towards the window, watching the scene of the burial as if watching a play. Something pricked her attention. A figure set apart from the rest of the mourners, standing by a small tree. Mary squinted to get a better look as the carriage drew nearer, cutting through the landscape as the body was lowered into it.

'Percy, look!' She pointed outside.

'What am I looking at?' Percy asked.

'That figure.'

'Must be one of the mourners.' He shrugged, leaning back into his seat.

'No, I did not see them at the church.' Mary's mind raced through the faces she had seen during the service; they had not been there.

The carriage sped on, the scene of the burial flickering into perfect view for a split-second before it was behind them. Mary gasped.

'Percy, *that* is the chimney sweep who was at the wedding!'

Claire flexed her fingers, sighed, and played the piece of music again. The notes were swimming on the page like angry tadpoles and she had long since stopped caring whether she was keeping time. It didn't seem to matter what she did, nothing was right for Lady Mawdsley, who winced and grabbed the side of her chair every time Claire started the tune.

'No, no, no, that wasn't right either.'

Claire ducked, successfully dodging the latest scrunched-up ball of paper, which landed on the floor beside her with all the others.

'What was wrong that time?' Claire asked, aware of Lady Mawdsley's frosty glare.

'It felt too fast. This accompanies — which of the poems was it again?'

Claire closed her eyes; she didn't need to look any more. '"She Walks in Beauty".' Even the title gave her goosebumps and allowed her to believe that Byron had written it about her, though they had yet to meet.

'I need to be word perfect, and you need to be note perfect for the concert on Tuesday.'

Claire stopped playing. '*I* need to be note perfect? I thought I was merely helping you to learn the tunes and the words to the songs?'

'That was the original plan but seeing how you've learnt the songs so successfully —' Lady Mawdsley paused for long enough to shake her head and sigh, which signified her unspoken but bitter disappointment before resuming — 'I have decided that you will do.'

Claire had dreaded this moment — the one where she would come face to face with her idol Byron in circumstances of someone else's making. She would much prefer to meet him on neutral territory, somewhere she could at least try to be enigmatic and interesting; not introduced as the poor companion to a cantankerous, parchment-throwing grand dame. From the rumours she'd heard about him, Byron was quick to form attachments but quicker to lose interest, and he was now a married man, which dashed all but the smallest thread of hope. Besides, Claire wanted to meet him as an equal. There was nothing for it, she would have to make up an illness or family emergency that would get her out of playing that evening — although to do so would risk Lady Mawdsley ending her employment and her chances of getting Lord Byron's attention.

'Would it not seem a little —' Claire clasped her hands together, perfecting her most earnest expression as she spoke, knowing full well where the knife would pierce — '*amateurish* if I were to accompany you? You who have recited the works of Wordsworth and Tennyson at the theatres? You who have been the darling of the theatrical world, who has known rapturous applause, held the audience in your hand?' Claire watched Lady Mawdsley play out the disappointment in her head, she could practically see the seeds of doubt she'd planted take hold. Lady Mawdsley, who lived for approval, playing out the scenario where the wolves of polite society tore apart her evening, making her the laughing stock of every social gathering of the ton.

'It is only a small gathering of ourselves, the Byron household and a few select others, not *King Lear*.' Lady Mawdsley folded her arms as she regained her composure. She worked her jaw. Claire's plan had backfired. The old woman had more steel in her than Claire had imagined. *Think, think*. Her next steps were crucial. She had to somehow shift the responsibility onto someone else, someone whose good opinion Lady Mawdsley craved.

'Byron has given you an advance copy of the poems and music, has he not?' Claire continued. 'I am sure he will be delighted by *any* recitation of the verses, however clumsily executed. But I am not a professional and I know first-hand how sensitive poets are, how easily offended.'

'You think that Lord Byron would shun *me* because of *your* poor skills?'

'I am fearful of it.' Claire bit her lip.

Lady Mawdsley strummed her fingers on the top of the folio of poems.

'He *is* very sensitive.' Lady Mawdsley nodded. 'He once stormed out of a dinner party because someone called *Childe Harold*, *Child Maud*. He was furious.'

'Imagine if he did that here? What about Persephone?'

Claire knew bringing the dog into the argument was a masterstroke. Lady Mawdsley cared nothing for Claire's feelings, but she reserved all her care and love for that walking curtain.

'Persephone is very delicate and very dear. Perhaps I could engage a concert room and make the celebration bigger. Byron would love that; he is such a peacock and to have the eyes of the ton feasting on him…'

Lady Mawdsley fell into a brief reverie, Claire wondered what pictures flew through the old lady's daydreams; perhaps they were the same as hers? Could you imagine! She snorted at the idea, quickly disguising it with a gentle cough that burst through whatever dream Lady Mawdsley was having.

'Yes, I will do that. Claire, you are dismissed.'

'What?' Claire squeaked. This wasn't the result she was expecting.

'Not from your position, you simpleton, from the concert.' Lady Mawdsley shook her head. 'Fetch a quill and some paper, we will make a list of suitable venues and pianists, and you will find me a suitable alternative.'

As Claire got up from the piano, she permitted herself the smallest of smiles. A new plan was emerging in her mind and Lady Mawdsley had not only given her the idea, but she had also given her the means of executing it. All she had to do now was ensure that Augusta would not accompany them to the event, otherwise her cover would be blown.

'You are sure you will not accompany me this evening?' Lady Mawdsley took Claire's hand as she stepped into the carriage. The venue was only minutes away, but Lady Mawdsley did not walk anywhere — preferring to make a dramatic entrance wherever she went.

'My head is swimming and I feel sick. I would hate to ruin your evening and draw attention away from the show if I were to be taken ill.'

Lady Mawdsley shuddered at the thought.

'Well, if you feel as unwell as all that, you must go back to the house.' Lady Mawdsley shrugged, any sympathy well disguised by obvious irritation. 'I will sit with Lord and Lady Byron; they always take good care of me.'

Lady Mawdsley smoothed the rug across her knees, tucking herself into the grand carriage that dwarfed her.

'I hope you have a good evening.' Claire smiled and stepped back as the door to the carriage was closed. She watched the carriage rumbled off into the distance. Having put one part of her plan into action — the accelerated intimacy with Augusta; first the walk in the park, then the invitation to tea and the herb in the tea to cause a stomach-ache — it was time to initiate the second part, preventing Augusta from attending the event by adding a herb to her tea to induce sickness.

Claire rushed back into the house, racing up the stairs at a pace that roused Persephone and made the dog utter drowsy barks from her basket. She opened her wardrobe and took out the one expensive dress she owned, the one that would shield her true identity and maybe, just maybe, convince Lord Byron that she was worthy of attracting his interest.

Timing it with military precision, Claire got ready and sped along to the venue just as the audience spilled out. Having played the tunes so often, she knew the order of them in her sleep; she had predicted when they would have an interval for refreshments and also knew exactly where the Byrons and Lady Mawdsley would be sitting. She could see Lady Mawdsley and Lady Byron from the corner of her eye, still in their seats, but the third seat in their box — the one reserved for Lord Byron — was empty, so it was easy to deduce that he had left to soak up the adoration of the audience.

Claire scanned the crowd of immaculately dressed people, the women scattered across the room like different coloured flowers. There he was. Claire's pulse raced at the sight of him leaning against a red and gold wall, even the curls on the wallpaper curved towards him, trying to touch him with circular fronds. All the other men looked dull and insipid compared to him; he was perfection, as if chiselled by the gods. Claire could do nothing more than stare, allowing herself to commit every aspect of his face to memory; the black curls of his hair that he kept pushing away from his face, the strong jawline that he showcased by tipping his head back in laughter, the porcelain skin at his throat with the Adam's apple bobbing like a conker in the middle. She felt a sudden urge to kiss it. It was easy to see why people lost themselves when he was around, in this precise moment he could ask Claire to do — or be — anything and she would say yes. He saw her and for a brief, delicious moment that felt like an eternity, their eyes met and locked. Claire felt a rush of sensation charging towards her like an army of horses, she closed her eyes to steady herself and when she opened them again Byron was in front of her.

'Good evening.' Byron nodded. 'Are you feeling ill? You looked like you might faint.' His lip curled up at the side, he clearly expected young women to swoon in his presence.

'No, thank you.' Claire steadied herself. 'I am not ill, I am late, that is all.'

'You have missed the first half of the recital, Lady …?'

'Lady Upton.' Claire curtseyed, a slight wobble in her left ankle as she regained her posture telling her that maybe she wasn't as stable as she'd thought.

'I am George Byron, Lord George Byron. Perhaps you have heard of me?'

'Is it better if I have or have not?' Claire smirked.

'Better to be prepared and to feign ignorance.'

'Prepared for what?'

Claire looked down, she had to, his gaze was electrifying her like one of Galvani's frogs.

'Wait outside when the recital has finished, I would like to talk with you again.' His lips were almost touching her ear, his breath a fire against her skin. Claire was almost relieved to look up and see his receding figure, his tailcoat fanning out behind him like a peacock's plume. She breathed out, suddenly realising she had been holding her breath.

She crept into the room and took a seat at the back, as far removed from Lady Mawdsley as she could manage. As Claire predicted, the poems were infinitely better with the addition of a professional musician and the poet himself made a more than adequate substitute for Lady Mawdsley, though Claire found herself missing Lady Mawdsley's dramatic rolling of letters and elongated pauses between verses. Claire's heart swelled, she had done it; she had finally met Lord Byron and not only that, he had asked her to meet him after the performance. This gave her something of a quandary: to meet him again was an agreement to whatever fleeting, physical delights he had planned, and though it was tempting to give in to her body's yearning for him, Claire knew it was not a path to longevity. No, it was far better to leave it as a tantalising glimpse of desire, ignite the flame and start the game of cat and mouse, to make herself so unobtainable that to obtain her becomes an all-encompassing desire. Of course, there was a huge fault in this plan. Byron had women — and men — throwing themselves at him all the time, so it was highly likely that he would forget about Lady Upton as soon as he cast his eyes on another suppliant, beautiful woman.

Claire's mind chewed over all the possible endings to the evening before she decided on the one that would make the biggest impression. It was not something that would be expected of a woman in Lady Upton's position, but seeing how that was as much a reinvention as Claire's latest name, she figured she had nothing to lose. Poets loved graveyards and if Byron was anything like Shelley he would find the environs of death and decay a place of tumescence and growth. They would get carried away but not *too* carried away, and he would leave the place in such a state that her name would linger on his lips and he would be desperate to see her again.

Resolved of her plan, Claire allowed her mind to drift into the fantasies as she watched Byron recite the second part of the 'Hebrew Melodies'. Shutting her eyes, allowing herself to be swept away with the music, her breathing slowed to match the gentle pacing of the verse. The clapping crowd awoke her, and she joined in with their rapturous applause before making her way out of the room, hiding around the corner of the theatre as the audience trickled out onto the streets or into waiting carriages.

Lady Mawdsley and Lady Byron were the last to get into carriages, the latter getting into a large black carriage bedecked with golden trims and Byron's initials emblazoned with a regal style crest on the side of it. She looked pale and fragile against the dual blackness of the carriage and the abrupt nightfall. Claire's heart sank at the trickery she had adopted to prevent Byron's sister joining them, but it swelled again as she thought of her success — Byron had asked to meet her, he had noticed her and wanted to see her again. That was all that needed to be remembered.

The cool breeze fortified Claire's senses and firmed her resolve. Byron had long been the subject of her heart's desire and all her romantic quests had been merely stepping stones to this opportunity, she would not mess it up now. She looked up at the moon, full and brilliant, shining its approval on her and casting her in what she already knew to be a flattering light. The sound of footsteps behind her made her heart race, and she took a deep breath before turning around.

'You came?' Byron's voice glided on the night sky, the darkness of his features shadowed by the moon. He was so close to her she could feel his chest against hers. A bat flapped noisily past them, and Claire jumped back, resting her back against the cool stone of the theatre. Byron had loosened his shirt and the unbuttoned cravat rested on either side of his collarbones. She wanted to trace the skin with her finger like the map of an undiscovered country.

'Shall we take a walk, *Lady Upton*?'

The way he said her name confirmed he was under no illusion that it was her real one; but he was here, so that was sign enough that he was willing to play along. Claire put her arm through his and he tightened his grip around it as they walked through the theatre district.

'Shall we go to the graveyard?' she said, boldly.

Byron raised his eyebrows. 'The graveyard? Do you suppose poets yearn to be among the dead to bring their words to life?'

'I find a graveyard a wonderful place for philosophising.' Claire quickened the pace, walking so quickly that her arm slid out of his and she did not slot it back into its former place. 'It is your mind I wish to share, Lord Byron, not your body.'

Now she had said the words aloud, she was surprised by their truth. It was exactly how she felt. Desire had not abated, but she knew it was fleeting. Claire wanted a future with Byron, not a memory. She wanted something tangible and meaningful, something as strong and timeless as the stone monuments they headed towards. Byron hesitated, his eyes flashing.

'I thought the terms of this agreement were understood. I do not need a woman to philosophise with, I have books and friends enough for that.'

Claire's illusions shattered. He was practically stamping his feet, his brow furrowed into the cross expression of a child told he could not have another toy. How quickly his mood had shifted from romantic lover to obstinate man, how ordinary he seemed.

'Well, it appears we have both been misled. Goodnight.'

Claire walked off, her steps automatically turned toward Piccadilly Terrace, but she couldn't go back there, not while he was several paces behind. The moon had all but disappeared now, casting the night sky in a sheath of total blackness that made the familiar streets into strangers, and Claire's heart beat a loud, warning drum in her ears.

'Where are you going?' he shouted. 'It is not safe for a lady to be walking alone at night.'

Great, Claire thought, *now he's worried about social convention. He wasn't so concerned with that when he wanted to indulge in some amorous congress.* She carried on walking, panic propelling her forward. Though she did not quite know where she was going now, she had taken a path off the main route back to Lady Mawdsley's house.

'Suit yourself, I will retire to my gentleman's club. Good night!'

Claire stopped. Byron's footsteps bid a hasty retreat down the side alley which provided the gateway to the places of the night and the women of ill-repute who would have no sudden changes of heart and would lick whatever wounds were put before them, if enough gold coins were offered. She closed her eyes, shaking her head at her stupidity. What devilment had made her think she could construct such a plan, let alone enact it? She had no experience in matters of romance and no experience of men other than what she had gleaned from Mary's romance with Percy. How typical that she should completely mess up the one chance she had. How foolish she had been! If she was going to play it meek and mild and try to feign intellectual equanimity, she should have allowed Lady Mawdsley to conduct a private recital at her house and played the piano well enough for her skills to be noted and her demeanour to be enchanting. Now there was no hope of looking alluring or any of the other qualities she had feigned to possess; now she looked deranged, inconsistent, and plain odd — all qualities she would ascribe to her actual self.

Eventually, Claire reached Lady Mawdsley's house. Her legs burned with the effort of her quickened pace and her dress clung to the sweat on her back. In the morning, she would be forced to listen to Lady Mawdsley crowing about how much of a success the evening had been, and she would have to swallow down her own feelings. The back door was open, just as she had left it, and Claire crept silently into the house, closing and locking the door behind her. She jolted at the sight of Lady Mawdsley's white statues blanched to the colour of bone in the moonlight. Claire made her way up the stairs, careful to side-step the stair that creaked, stepped out of her dress, and left it in a puddle on the floor as she made her way into bed.

Sleep would not come, and Claire thought back to happier times, hoping it would relax her mind and free her up to sleep. The heat of summer in Paris warmed her bones and she could once again feel the heavy weight of the chest as they carried it while Percy rode Napoleon the donkey through the hazy countryside. She thought of the person she had been then, and the excitement and willingness she felt to cast everything aside and live in the moment buzzed afresh within her. But where had that left her? Ostracised from Mary because she did not know how to deal with her sister's sadness over the death of the baby; one false move after another when she thought she was doing the right thing and helping them all heal. Getting closer to Percy had not been intentional, but as Mary had pushed him away, Claire had worried that any further break would be irreversible, and Mary would find herself cast out of his affections as brutally as Harriet had been previously. In Claire's mind, it had been better for her to take him as a lover than for Percy to seek companionship elsewhere. The first time they had slept together had felt more like a confession than passion, and it had only happened twice before their relationship reverted to what it had always been: a friendship.

Claire's relationship with Percy had been a turning point for them both; convincing Claire that Percy was not the man for her and convincing Percy that he needed to make amends with Mary. He had taken her away for a couple of days after their romantic relationship had ended and, although Claire wasn't proud of her actions with the bonfire, it had united them in the shared belief that they would be better off without her. Burning Percy's poems and the baby's things had been intended to cleanse herself of all the ghosts in her own heart, she had not dreamt that they would come back from their trip and see her actions as some sort of sacrifice.

Claire tucked herself up in a ball as the guilt and the sorrow flowed through her. All she could hope was that one day Mary would forgive her. Whatever else these past weeks had taught her, one thing was abundantly clear — she missed her sister.

CHAPTER TEN

'The evening was a tremendous success,' Lady Mawdsley boomed over breakfast. 'It is a shame you missed it; everyone was there.'

Claire hid her smile behind her teacup. It had been a good idea to take charge of the guest list, for it meant that Claire could name all the attendees and the imaginary guests whose names she had added to the list. Now she had passed through the darkness of her guilt about Mary and Percy and the morning dawn had faded all fears that she'd done the wrong thing with Byron, she felt a glowing sense of pride that she hadn't acted on desire but had dropped enough tantalising glimpses of it to spark his interest. Of course, it could all still go horribly wrong, and Lady Upton be written off by Byron as a bad bet, but that was the advantage of a fictional identity; she always had her true self to fall back on and Claire Clairmont hadn't met him yet.

'Lord Byron is such a gentleman. He could see that my throat was becoming hoarse after the first recital, so he took to the stage himself to take over the reading.'

Claire bit her lip. Much better to let Lady Mawdsley rest in her delusion; more likely he could not stand to see his words butchered by her and stormed the stage before she could murder another stanza.

'You look ghastly this morning, even paler than usual. Are you still plagued by that headache?' Lady Mawdsley wagged a knife at Claire, whose eyes were drawn to the slither of ham that clung to it like a piece of skin.

'No, it has passed, but I did not sleep well.'

'A long walk in the park with Persephone will perk you up.' The ham made its way to Lady Mawdsley's mouth and her attempts to chew it were met with some resistance, the ham frequently bobbing up to Lady Mawdsley's lips like someone waiting to be saved. Claire turned her head away at the sight. A walk with Persephone would get her out of the firing line of Lady Mawdsley's questions and boasts about Byron. Some consolation was given by the fact Lady Mawdsley knew nothing of the fictitious Lady Upton.

'Is she to go in the chair or use her feet?' Claire asked.

'The chair, of course,' came Lady Mawdsley's stern response.

Claire got the chair ready and placed Persephone's cushion atop it. There were probably hundreds of people in London with genuine need of a chair such as this, and yet Lady Mawdsley used it to transport a lazy dog around London's parks. Anger at the frivolity of it swirled in Claire's stomach. She patted the seat, and the dog looked up at her as if asking 'Yes, and how do you expect me to get up there?' Claire rolled her eyes, scooped the dog up, and plonked her into the chair. Persephone made herself comfortable on the cushion before looking at Claire again.

'Come on then, Cleopatra, let's go.'

The chair bounced against the steps as she lowered it down onto the cobbled pavement in front of the house. Stopping to breathe a sigh of relief at being away from Lady Mawdsley, a tap on her shoulder made Claire jump. It was Augusta.

'You two are out early this morning.'

'I could say the same about you.' Claire pushed the dog down the road towards the park.

'Yes, well, I wanted to get out of the house. George is in a foul mood, stomping around like a bear.' Augusta shook her head. 'He did not come home until the break of dawn and there were such harsh words thrown between him and Annabella. I got dragged into it all, as I always do.' Her shoulders sunk with a resignation Claire recognised. 'My visit was *supposed* to be a holiday and a brief one at that, they both use me as a referee in their pugilist contests; but they jab with words, not blows.'

'It sounds hideous. I perfectly understand your need to escape from it. You are safe here, there is nothing but a spoilt dog and an underpaid companion. Our conversations are sacred, there will be nothing to referee, only the talk of the ton. Tell me, how did the recital go?'

'Badly, I suspect, from George's need to get drunk afterwards.'

'Did you not attend?'

'No, I felt sick and stayed at home. I was glad of the peace, to be honest with you, Jane. It was a good thing I rested too, as I got little rest when George came home.'

'I do not wish to pry, Augusta, but talking might remove the burden from your shoulders. But, if you would rather, we can turn the conversation to lighter things, like Lady Mawdsley's false teeth.' A ripple of disgust ran through Claire's body. Augusta laughed and pressed her hand on Claire's arm.

'Tell me more of Lady Mawdsley's teeth, a good laugh will be the perfect antidote to my melancholy.'

They circled the empty park, Claire regaling Augusta with tales of Lady Mawdsley — she had not realised she had accrued so many. As they walked, the park became populated with nannies pushing babies, and people scuttling through on their way to work or house-calls. The trees had sprung into life, bathing in the golden glow of the sunshine that was slow to get going this morning, but rewarded the sky with opulence as a reward for its tardiness. When Persephone snored from the chair, too tired to bark at birds in flight or the ducks on the pond, it was time to go home.

Augusta took a deep breath as she looked back at the terrace.

'Are you sure you wouldn't like to call on Lady Mawdsley?' said Claire. 'I am sure she would be delighted to tell you all about last night.'

'No, thank you, Jane. I heard enough of it through the bedroom walls.'

'I am sure Lord Byron has awoken in a much calmer temper.' Claire smiled.

'I feel much fortified by our conversation and ready for anything.' Augusta's responding smile spread across her face. 'Thank you for your wise counsel, Jane, I feel blessed that you came into my life.'

Something about the fact she'd given Augusta her old name made Claire's stomach tense as she negotiated Persephone in her chair up the steps to the house. Augusta poured her heart out to her, and she had only used her to find out more about Byron. Claire had never had any friendships that were not rooted in family or jealousy — or both — perhaps she did not know what it meant to be genuine. Was it too late to tell Augusta the truth? After all, it was only a name — or a couple of names. The wheels caught on the step; Claire tugged at the chair and Persephone growled at the sudden movement. If only Lady Mawdsley would let her use the rear entrance to the house which had no steps or obstacles to entry, it would be so much simpler, but she had looked horrified at the mere suggestion of entering through the tradesman's entrance.

Claire hesitated as she opened the front door and heard laughter. Laughter meant company. She closed the door gently behind her, trying desperately not to make a noise. Perhaps she could put Persephone in the library and take herself upstairs and out of the way without being discovered.

'Claire, is that you?'

Lady Mawdsley's friendly tone — the one she only ever used when she had visitors whom she wished to impress.

'Yes, Lady Mawdsley. Shall I put Persephone in the library?'

'No, no, bring her to me. There is someone I would like you to meet.'

Claire looked in the mirror, smoothed down her hair and took a deep breath; which one of Lady Mawdsley's society friends had come to dissect the evening's performance? Slowly she walked into the morning room. Lady Mawdsley had positioned herself on the chair beside the window, the one which caught the morning sun and illuminated her features — another sign that Lady Mawdsley was out to impress. Her guest's identity was swamped by a tall chair that usually lived in the dining room, its opulent red curves standing out against the muted greens and golds of the room.

Perhaps it was her stepfather William Godwin or — worse still — her mother, finally discovering that she'd taken paid employment not two leagues from their house. Her throat went dry, and she swallowed as Lady Mawdsley beckoned her forward.

'Claire has been dying to meet you, ever since you kindly gave us the advanced folio.'

Claire froze. She knew exactly who was in that chair and he was the last person she wanted, or expected, to see.

An arm gripped the side of the chair, a head of dark curly hair swung around to face her. Byron's eyes widened as he looked at her, his mouth dropping open momentarily before it turned into a smirk.

'Claire Clairmont, this is Lord Byron.'

Claire dropped an awkward curtsey in Byron's direction, which made Lady Mawdsley tut and shake her head.

'Sit down and pour us some more tea and then you may pour some for yourself. Claire has literary links too, George. Have you heard of the Shelley scandal?'

Byron pouted. 'No, I cannot say that I have. I rarely give time to idle chatter — being so often on the receiving end of it myself — but do tell me about this one, Lady Mawdsley, I find myself fascinated by it.'

He leant back in the chair, his eyes fixed on Claire as she tried desperately to hold the rattling teapot.

'Well.' Lady Mawdsley clapped her hands on her knees. 'Percy Shelley was married to a young woman called Harriet, and they had a child together. A girl, wasn't it? Or perhaps there were two?'

Claire remained silent. Lady Mawdsley was talking as if the story was about some unknown persons, not Claire's own family. How she wished she could put a large dose of arsenic in her employer's tea.

'And then,' Lady Mawdsley continued, pausing only to take the tea that Claire handed to her, 'then he met Claire's sister Mary Godwin, and they eloped to Paris, leaving poor Harriet pregnant and bereft. Claire went along with them, didn't you, Claire?'

'Really?' Byron's eyes flashed with interest. 'I would like to meet Shelley; I am a great admirer of *Queen Mab*.' As Claire passed him a cup, his hand brushed against hers. 'And Mary Godwin is the daughter of Mary Wollstonecraft, is she not? What a wonderful woman she was.'

Claire sat through a painful rendition of the previous night's activities and was relieved when Lady Mawdsley implored her to move to the piano so they might show Lord Byron the fruits of their labours. He watched Claire like a hawk and her fingers felt clumsy and heavy, refusing to land where she aimed them. She had missed several notes — for which she would be berated by Lady Mawdsley later — when the temptation to look at him overwhelmed her. Whatever had passed between them last night had carried over to the day, and Claire was almost relieved that her earlier contrivance had been called out. At least all was in the open and whatever happened from this point forward — and the way he was watching her left her in no uncertain terms that something would happen — would all be from a point of total honesty. Well, perhaps not *total* honesty.

When it was time for him to go, Lady Mawdsley asked Claire to see him out. The effort of entertaining had been exhausting and she was expecting another round of visitors that afternoon, so she bid Byron farewell and turned her chair towards the sun, ready for her nap. As the door closed behind them, Claire felt Byron's hand upon her arm, scorching through the fabric of her dress and making her veins pulse.

'I have it on good authority that you are acquainted with a friend of mine, a Lady Upton?'

Claire coughed. 'Yes, I believe I have had the pleasure of meeting her.'

'Perhaps you would be good enough to ask her to write to me, I have a matter I would like to discuss with her.'

'I will do that,' Claire stammered. 'But I do not have an address for her.'

'It is no matter.' Byron shrugged. 'If you are happy to act as go-between, I will get my houseboy to drop the letters here to you. Would that be acceptable?'

Claire could not stop herself from smiling. 'That would be most acceptable.'

'Capital.' Byron smiled, holding her gaze just long enough to light the tinder that flickered constantly in the pit of her being. He took her hand and kissed it. 'I will see you soon, Lady Upton.'

Doddingley was out of sight, but not out of mind as far as Mary was concerned. What a strange community it was. What poor taste for another chimney sweep to attend the funeral, taking on the same clothing and aspect as Thomas Lakin. Though Percy had claimed not to see the figure of the chimney sweep, she knew what she had seen. It could not have been a trick of the light. It *was* a person, just like the chimney sweep at the wedding. Everything about him was the same, from the height of the broom to the patches of soot disguising his face. The carriage had only passed them for a moment, but it was long enough for her to be certain about what she saw. But, then again, sometimes when she closed her eyes she could see beloved Clara and find herself back in that room rubbing the heat back into her daughter's hands. Could she really believe anything she thought she saw?

A long summer continued well into September clinging on to its earlier promise, Windsor Park bloomed spectacularly with fragrant flowers and sheltering trees and Mary spent her afternoons idling on the bank or the river, reading and allowing the sunshine to fortify her and nourish the new life growing inside her. Percy knew of the pregnancy now and the nausea of the early stage passed into a state of habitual serenity; Percy's delight at the news and his unfailing optimism had forced her to relax into pregnancy and allow herself to believe that this time, the outcome would be different.

There had been another boost to her mood too, since returning to Windsor, there had been letters from Adele and

Lilian; they helped to sustain Mary while the social life of London floated away from her. She had expected to hear from Claire but reasoned that the split between them was doing everybody a service — allowing each to find their own identities independent of the others. Percy had never written so much, and his days were spent to and froing with publishers or working on 'The Spirit of Solitude' — Mary cared little for the title of the work and hoped it would be relegated to a subtitle upon the book's publication.

At the end of another afternoon in Windsor Park, Mary made her way back to Bishopsgate, winding through the green boughs, the soft lake rushing to her as if willing her not to leave. A letter awaited her; Lilian's decorative curls swept across the page and into her heart. To know that their friendship was, if not restored, then at least resumed had thawed her feelings towards Reginald Ullmann, convincing her that his had warmed towards her. *Friendship is the most vital thing in the world*, Mary thought to herself as she opened the letter and sat down on the settle to read it. *A lover may make you feel you are the centre of their world, but with friends you have a world to be the centre of.* She settled in, preparing for more anecdotes of rural life. The news of Lilian's pregnancy had come as a shock, even more of a shock to discover it was far more advanced than her own. She prayed that all would go smoothly with the birth.

Mary hurried through the letter; this was the way she always approached them — scanning them first to delight in the overarching themes of the letter then reading it more closely to savour in its detail. It was like eating a delicious morsel of food, much better to savour than devour. Exactly as predicted, the letter chronicled the final stages of her pregnancy, but while the other letters had been upbeat, this one felt different. Lilian sounded — haunted. There was no other word for it. She read the letter through again, trying to pinpoint the meanings behind it.

My pregnancy continues well; my stomach is as large as a ball and just as tiresome to carry. People tell me it must be a boy because it is all contained to the front. The period of my confinement draws near, and my dreams are plagued by such horrendous visions that have seeped into my days, staining even my waking moments with their monstrous hue.

I dream — and I can scarcely write this for my hand is shaking so — I dream terrible things will happen during my confinement. It always goes the same way: I am alone in bed and the room is in darkness without a candle or sunlight to warm it. There are no sounds except the sound of my slumber. I think there is a baby there, but I can only fumble in the dark for its crib. A slice of light underneath the door sparks my curiosity, and I leave the room. When I walk down the corridor, I hear voices, Reginald — I think — and some of the other men from the village; perhaps the other men from the Farmer's Council. They are laughing about something among themselves. They do not see me at first, but when they do, their laughter stops and they turn to me with foaming mouths, snarling like a pack of dogs. I turn to run, leaving the house, and run over the hill into the village, but they are on the scent, hunting me down. I try each house in the village, but the faces of each occupant have taken on the same shape — feasting hounds. I run and run until I can run no more, but they do not let up from their chase. I pause when I realise I must go back for the baby, that I cannot leave it to this braying mob, but the hounds are upon me and I awake, drenched with sweat.

Mary, you are the only person wise enough to tell me what this means? Am I hysterical, or is it a warning?

'Well, Percy, what do you think?'

'I think Lilian has been eating too much cheese before bedtime.' Percy sat back. 'It is only natural for women to get a little emotional in confinement. I myself would have nightmares if I were to be stuck in a room for weeks.'

'Let us be grateful then that your contribution took the form it did.' They giggled at the thought. 'In all seriousness, it is not like Lilian to share this; she must be terrified.'

'Perhaps living in that odd little village has finally taken its toll. She is accustomed to more civilised places; the dream is reminding her she feels like a stranger there.'

'But she and Reginald have such a grand life in Doddingley, the entire village is in thrall of them both. How could she feel like an outsider?'

'Remember the dreams that you had after the death of Clara?' Percy spoke carefully. Mary's heart twisted at the reminder, but she took a deep breath and nodded.

'I know you are right; pregnancy and childbirth are terrifying; it is no wonder the brain should make its own monsters to dance with those real terrors.'

'Write to her, tell her she is not alone, reassure her the dreams will pass when the baby is born, and that all will be well. Doubtless she will stop seeing the villagers as bloodthirsty hounds then.'

Percy kissed Mary on the head before leaving the room, leaving Mary to contemplate all that he had said. The terrors of pregnancy and confinement could bring on any manner of spectacular visions, but what if there was something behind it, something that Lilian feared but could not quite name? What if she had seen or overheard something that made her fearful?

Mary raced to her desk, drawing out the notebook and map she had squirrelled away upon their return to Bishopsgate. She flicked through the pages, re-reading the testimonies, looking for something — anything — that would knot her suspicions together. After Percy had dismissed her sighting of the chimney sweep at the burial, she had told no one else about it, but perhaps she could ask Adele and Lilian, see what they had to say? If they could confirm that there was a chimney sweep there, even if it didn't turn out to be Lakin, at least that would rid her mind of this ridiculous notion that there was some sort of conspiracy going on, that the coincidence of the two deaths in quick succession could be something more.

She slumped down onto the settle. What was it about Reginald Ullmann that made her so determined to cast him as a murderer? Now that he had relaxed his grip on Lilian, surely, she could turn her mind to gratitude and stop looking for something that wasn't there. Mary sighed, throwing the notebook down. There was nothing in any of the testimonies to paint Reginald as anything more than an average landlord. What was more, Lilian loved him and was about to have his child. Mary put her head in her hands and massaged her temples. It was time to clear her own thoughts and write a comforting letter to Lilian.

CHAPTER ELEVEN

Claire ran for the post as usual; the housekeeper had been glad to rescind this task when Claire had proposed it be added to her list of duties. After all, she was the one reading out the letters to Lady Mawdsley, so it stood to reason that she should be the one to receive them. Of course, she had an ulterior motive, as the summer months had brought a flurry of letters to Lady Upton from Lord Byron, increasing during their month-long retreat to the countryside, where the dull Shropshire landscape was enlivened by the sparks of Byron's personality that leapt off the page and up to her waiting lips as she kissed the parchment and dreamed of him.

Now she was back in Piccadilly Terrace. Their proximity and the differences in their social standing that kept them apart brought with it a new frisson which — coupled with Lady Byron's difficult pregnancy and the nagging presence of his sister — made the enigmatic Lady Upton a tantalising prospect. Claire had been careful to ensure her letters were not those of a love-struck fantasist and had undertaken painstaking research on the gentle art of persuasion from the classics of literature and mythology. Though she would not call herself worldly and did not possess Mary's ability to sum up a person's entire character from the scantest of acquaintance, Claire felt she had the measure of Byron — even if her vision was impaired by her endless adoration which their correspondence fuelled.

But it wasn't the letter from Byron that surprised her this morning, it was a letter in another hand, a familiar, sisterly one. Claire stared at the letter, the soft brushstrokes of Mary's pen exuding her usual calm and warmth, with no trace of fire. Perhaps it was an invitation to reside with them once more in Windsor? Claire's heart sank at the prospect, and she knew in that moment that she would never live with them again. Now she had got used to Lady Mawdsley's eccentric ways, she enjoyed the freedom from familial dramas and even Persephone had snuggled a way into Claire's affections. Now she did not notice the snickers and incredulous faces as she wheeled the dog around the park; now she was almost proud to be seen with her.

'Bring me my letters.'

Lady Mawdsley had the hearing of a fox for anything Claire wished to conceal.

'Right away, Lady Mawdsley.' Claire kissed the letter from Byron and pushed it down her neckline, next to her heart. She held the other letters in her hand and walked to Lady Mawdsley, a sudden longing to hear what Mary had to say taking a slow bloom in her heart.

Later, once the business of Persephone's walk and Lady Mawdsley's letters, lunch and afternoon recitation had been dealt with, Claire closed the door on her employer's slumbering form, escaping up to her room to read the letters. Usually she would tear at Byron's with the speed she'd like to tear at his breeches, but Mary's letter intrigued her in a different way and she opened it carefully, biting her lip as she unfurled it. Mary's words did not leap from the page as Byron's did, nor did they add tinder to a growing fire; instead, they were words of consolation and kindness, a sharing of a life with a sister's underlying tenderness. The words enveloped her into a hug: Mary's gentle sardonic humour making her laugh and the news of the pregnancy filling her with joy and sympathy for the fear that Mary must wrestle alongside her happiness. It ended with an invitation to tea at Windsor. Claire put her hand to her chest and sighed. No awkward questions about moving back, nothing more than cordiality and affection. She would accept the invitation and be delighted to do so.

Mary knew that writing to Claire was risky, her relationship with Percy had only just resumed its former footing and she knew that bringing Claire back into their lives could drive a wedge between them, as it had before. But things were different now and the perpetual winter that followed Clara's death had now caught pace with the natural step of the seasons and Mary had even felt the warmth of the autumn sun on her face and revelled in the gilded fingers of the leaves turning the trees to jewels.

She put her hand to her stomach, feeling reassured by the swell beneath it. The bump was already twice the size of Clara and staying still at Windsor — except for the early visitation to Doddingley — had allowed them both to become acquainted quietly, finding a rhythm with each other that gave her hope that maybe this time the result would be different.

'There.' She stepped back and admired the table she had put together. Granted, the cook had made the food, but Mary had put all the aspects of the high tea together. Her heart raced at the thought of seeing Claire again and a nervousness mixed with hope, she did not know how it would go. Polite and charming as she hoped it would all be, Mary could not halt the image of the bonfire and she doubted she would ever forget the look of satisfaction on Claire's face. Not five months earlier, she had set fire to everything that mattered to them. Did that hatred still burn within her? Had it dissipated into resentment? She had heard nothing from her in the intervening months, so it would be strange to be in touch again.

In truth, that was the real reason she had extended this invitation. Percy would no longer talk about Lilian and Reginald, feeling it to be an unhealthy obsession of Mary's. But the letter Lilian had sent about her nightmare had been followed by several more in the same vein, all throwing hints of unspoken fears. They were not worries about her confinement, or about the baby she would soon meet, but fears of the community and fears that the people around her were plotting and scheming something — but what? That is what the letters never said. After receiving the first, Mary had asked Percy if they could return to Doddingley, but he had rejected the request, calling it nothing more than an ill-placed hunch. He could see that Reginald was not a pleasant man, but he did not believe him to be a murderous one. Mary did not share his opinion and on the table behind the display of fruits, cakes and cheeses, she had hidden her notebook, the map they had made of Doddingley and all of Lilian's letters; hoping that Claire would interpret the case in the same way as she did.

'Miss Clairmont is here, madam. Shall I show her in?'

Mary jumped. 'Yes, of course. Sorry, I was daydreaming.'

She was always apologising to the staff; it came from a deep-rooted apology for having staff. Percy was all for the abolition of the class system, just as long as he could keep his comforts and privileges from it.

Claire stood in the doorway, and Mary gasped. She was so much changed that she would not have recognised her had she passed her in the street. Her hair was a darker chestnut brown than it had been months earlier, and the bags that had occupied the vacant spaces under her eyes had completely disappeared, giving her face a completely clear and dewy complexion like a pink pearl. That wasn't all. Her entire silhouette seemed different somehow, more womanly in the oddly conventional way of the time. Mary frowned.

'Are you wearing stays, Claire?'

'No social graces then, Mary?' Claire laughed. 'No polite hello or comment on how well I am looking, straight to the chase!'

When she smiled, she was beautiful. Staggering. Mary suddenly felt mousey and dull. Life as a paid companion was suiting Claire a little too well.

'You look so different,' Mary stammered. 'I cannot believe it.'

'Am I so very changed?' Claire looked at Mary, who felt the directness of the gaze as it travelled up and down her body, stamping it with disapproval. 'You are not. You look exactly the same and I am pleased to see it, it tells me that time has in some way restored you back to your former self.'

Mary did not know how to interpret Claire at the best of times, now she was out of practice for several months, she found it even harder to judge the presence of sincerity or sarcasm in her voice. Perhaps there were both, there usually was.

'I do feel better.' Mary took a deep breath. 'I am sorry for how I was with you after Clara's death, it was a bitter blow and one I had neither the tools nor the words to articulate.'

'I am glad you have been able to move forward.'

Moving forward, Mary thought, *but not forgetting.* She would never forget.

'I must congratulate you on your pregnancy. I expect Percy is thrilled.'

Mary stood to pour the tea, grateful that the action punctuated the conversation.

'He is.' She handed Claire the cup with a small smile.

'Good. I am glad.'

'And yourself? How is Lady Mawdsley?'

'Not so tiresome as you may think.' Claire tittered. 'I would almost say that I am growing quite fond of her and her ridiculous dog, Persephone.'

'She has a dog called Persephone?'

'She does.' Claire paused. Mary could sense that she was weighing up her next sentence. 'Did you know that Lord Byron and his wife live on the same terrace as Lady Mawdsley? Did you know that when you asked James to secure my employment there?'

Mary blushed. So Claire knew of her hand in the scheme.

'If we had stayed in the same house, Claire, we would have killed one another. I thought a separation would do us both good, and I was right.'

'That does not matter now.' Claire shrugged. 'I have always known that, and I agree with you. It is better that we live apart, but it would be nice if we could still be in each other's lives, would it not?'

'Yes,' Mary agreed, 'I think it would.' She sipped her tea. 'I did not know that Lord Byron lived there. Has it proved too much of a distraction for you?'

'Not in the slightest.' Claire smiled. 'I am kept so busy that I have barely met him.'

Mary knew that the sudden curve to Claire's lip meant she was not being entirely honest. There was no way she could live that close to Byron and not be hammering down the door with declarations of eternal devotion. She had talked enough of him when they had lived together — learning each of his poems by heart, knowing his every movement and interests with terrifying precision. Claire's adoration of Byron was well known and badly hidden, there was no way she could be in such proximity and do nothing. Claire was up to something, and Mary would discover what it was.

'It is good to be kept busy,' Mary started. 'I too have been rather busy, and I was wondering if you would help me with something.'

Mary told Claire everything that had passed in Doddingley, sparing no detail and eliciting such wide-eyed enthusiasm from Claire that the remainder of their tea went cold, and the cakes remained untouched.

'What delicious adventures you've been having without me.' Claire's eyes widened and she sat back in the chair, folding her arms.

'Well? What do you think about it all?'

'You are sure that the chimney sweep you saw at the graveside was the one who was at the wedding?'

'The costume of a chimney sweep does rather give them all a similar appearance…' Mary paused, she was backtracking, and she knew it. No, she was firm in her resolve when she first witnessed him, she would be firm now. 'Yes, I am sure of it. I did not see the body of Lakin, the runaway chimney sweep, but as far as I can tell, the man who was at the vicar's funeral was the same man at the wedding.'

'Have you asked Lilian about it?'

'I have and that's the curious thing, she says there wasn't a chimney sweep at the burial.'

'Might she not have noticed?'

'She is quite observant, so I think she would have seen him…'

'But Percy didn't?'

Mary stared at Claire with an expression that she hoped reflected their shared knowledge that Percy could not find a quill that was tickling the end of his nose.

'Perhaps he did not notice. Percy can lose a shoe when he is wearing them,' Claire agreed and the two stepsisters laughed in a way that brightened the room and unknotted the tension that Mary hadn't realised she'd carried in her shoulders.

'Your feeling is that Reginald had something to do with it?'

Mary nodded. 'I am almost sure of it.' There was something about Reginald that told her he wasn't the reasonable landlord the community thought him to be, but she could find no way of proving anything other than his unfair treatment of the owners of the Big House, and that was not an unusual move in the acquisition of property.

'Do you feel Lilian is in danger from him? Is that what her letters are saying?'

'Now that I don't know.' Mary sighed. Now that Lilian was about to become the mother of Reginald's child, there was no way that she would ever tell Mary directly of her fears or suspicions of her husband. 'Her letters are disturbing, but I cannot tell if it is her mind that is disturbed, the pregnancy playing tricks, or if there is genuine fear behind them and — if there is — who she is afraid of.'

'Let us have some more tea and look through the letters again,' Claire suggested. 'Will Percy be joining us soon?'

'No, Percy is in London on business. He is away for a few days. I am not expecting him back until Sunday.'

'Well, I shall stay long enough to solve this mystery, but I will not outstay my welcome.' Claire clapped her hands together. 'Back to business.'

*

The afternoon passed in an excited haze and when Mary closed the door on her sister; she had to admit that it had been a most enjoyable one. Perhaps she would ask James Berry to join her tomorrow. Having callers certainty put paid to the loneliness of creaking around in a house too big for one person, without another's laughter or conversation to thwart boredom. She had forgotten how good Claire's conversation could be, how enjoyable she was when in the right humour. Seeing each other sporadically might be enough to sustain a relationship in this note without the strains of over-familiarity or the necessity boredoms and frustrations of cohabitation gnawing away at it. She didn't believe a word Claire said about Byron, though; her smirk hinted at much more beneath the surface than Claire was willing to admit. Something was going on, Mary only hoped that Claire knew what she was doing. Rumours buzzed around Byron like a swarm of flies. It wasn't as though they themselves hadn't encountered enough rumours of their own, yet the last thing they needed was to attract any more.

Mary had the best night's sleep she'd had in weeks, reassured by Claire's belief in her assertions about the chimney sweep. She knew that there was only one thing she could do to fully put her mind at rest — she had to go back to the place where she had first met Lilian and Reginald. Dundee. If she hurried, she could arrange a carriage to arrive by the end of the week. The only problem was, she did not want to go alone and that meant she could either take a member of the household as a paid companion (and she couldn't imagine making arduous small talk over a long journey with the housekeeper or cook), ask James Berry and incur the many questions that would be aroused by a woman travelling with a man who wasn't her husband (even though Percy was only her husband by soul, not by holy matrimony), or her father, who was still not speaking to her. The candidates dwindled down to one — Claire.

She would catch the stagecoach on its return journey from Windsor to Ludgate Hill, taking rooms at La Belle Sauvage Inn before making its way to Piccadilly Terrace for Claire. Resolved of the plan, Mary put together a small case, taking money from Percy's desk and her notepad, pencil and map of Doddingley. Thankfully, the coach was on time and empty except for a woman and child who paid her no attention at all and spent the journey eating apples and talking about a grandfather's goat. Mary enjoyed dipping in and out of their conversation as if she were a bird flying down from a branch to investigate the ground below and, seeing nothing more beautiful than the tree, flying back up to it and staying there until a fresh curiosity took hold.

By the time the coach pulled up outside the inn it was late afternoon, and they were met by a line of faces belonging to travel-weary people awaiting the start of their journey to Windsor or Sherborne or Shrewsbury. If Claire agreed to the scheme, they would take the carriage from Fetter Lane and the White Horse Inn, which was infinitely more comfortable than this one. Mary made her way up a winding staircase that seemed to breathe in as she climbed the spindly steps to her room. A slow evening crowd was gathering in the inn below and Mary felt a tinge of vulnerability, which made her long for Percy's company and the protection of a man, although she knew that if it ever came to it, she would have no hesitation in using her pins, feet or fists to see off any attack.

There none and Mary collapsed onto a surprisingly comfortable bed, closing her eyes for a moment, and waking to a cheerful dark. Lighting the candle provided in the room, she unpacked the food she had brought from the house, eating her own apple and thinking of the companionship between the boy and his mother on the coach. She tried to imagine a future where she might be that woman telling her child to chew the apple rather than swallowing it in undigested clumps. Imagining her child's future made Clara's loss harder to bear, the notion that all those dreams had been snatched away before they had time to grow had stripped her to the bone, dismantling everything Mary knew of life and forcing her to rebuild herself like a scientist's monstrous invention. This baby would be her second chance, nothing would go wrong this time; there would be no nightmares of long passageways and empty cribs. Pushing the thoughts aside, she readied herself for bed and the early morning walk to Piccadilly Terrace.

CHAPTER TWELVE

'Nothing for months and then twice in as many days.' Claire was staggered when she opened the door to find Mary outside it. Persephone barked from the chair by the doorway where she was waiting, impatiently, for her morning walk.

'Is this Persephone?' Mary nodded towards the dog.

'Yes, yes, it is, and it is time for her early morning walk.'

'Who is at the door, Claire?'

Lady Mawdsley, proving once more that she did not miss a thing that did not concern her.

'A salesperson. They have the wrong house.'

'Well, hurry them along and take Persephone out. Close the door quickly, the draught is blowing in like an angry ghost.'

'An angry ghost?' Mary whispered. 'Do you have many angry ghosts calling here?'

'More than you'd suppose,' Claire hissed back. 'You can help me with this.'

Mary's jaw dropped when she saw Persephone's chariot. Claire remembered how her own had performed exactly the same action; but she was used to it now and looked forward to the strolls around the parks when London life was yawning itself awake or winding down, getting ready for the night. Once they were free of Lady Mawdsley's curiosity and hidden in the expanse of trees that covered them like golden umbrellas, Claire was ready to discover the reason for Mary's visit.

'I have come to see if you would like to accompany me on an adventure.'

'An adventure?' Claire's eyes narrowed. She knew to be sceptical of Mary's adventures, for they usually meant poking into someone else's business and putting themselves at risk. At least they would get a trip to Dundee out of it — after Mary's conversation yesterday there couldn't be another place she had in mind. 'The chimney sweep?'

'The chimney sweep.' Mary nodded. 'Percy would not entertain my going and meddling in Lilian's affairs, so I thought to take advantage of his absence.' Her face danced with mischievousness. 'What do you say? Can you fashion an escape from Lady Mawdsley?'

'Lady Mawdsley is herself going out of town this weekend and it is an event I am not invited to.' Claire feigned hurt. 'So I am at your disposal for detecting.' She clapped her hands excitedly, letting go of the chair's handles and sending it — and the dog — rushing down the slope with increasing speed. A quick, ungainly dash reunited Claire with a startled Persephone, who barked indignantly. Once Claire had got her breath back, she continued.

'Of course, I will have to wait until the carriage collects her at one o'clock, otherwise she will not let me go. If she thinks I have something more exciting to do than sit at home and walk Persephone, she will spoil it by insisting I travel with her.' Claire shrugged. 'That is the way her mind works.'

'The carriage leaves at three from Fetter Lane, do you know it?'

'No, but I can find it.'

'Pack lightly. I have not engaged a private carriage for us because I do not want Percy to learn of our plan.'

'But he will learn of it eventually?' Claire warned.

'Well, yes, he will, but by then we will have reprimanded the killer, so my actions will be justified.'

*

The journey to Dundee brought back memories of Mary's previous journey to Dundee two years earlier, though it looked very different from land. Back then, she had taken the packet from the Thames to the Tay, the sharp tang of salt in her nostrils, the sea waters casting up waves like hands to drag the travellers down into a watery grave. Much better to be on wheels than water, even if it took longer. It was essential for her to avoid the nausea that would remind her body of its morning sickness.

Dundee announced itself with flames cutting through the night sky of the docks, casting out the smell of gutted fish, unusable bones and burning tar. Tall towers of vats boiled whale skin into blubber and the harvest moon illuminated bones stacked like roofs sheltering the remains of discarded whales, seals, and walruses.

Mary and Claire reached the inn at ten o'clock with heavy eyelids and empty stomachs. A small supper of bread, milk and cheese was taken before they made their way up the dark staircase illuminated only by moonlight. It could have been a bed or a bale of hay for all they could see, but they were too tired to go back down and ask for light. Crawling onto the beds, sleep came quick as a fever, and both slumbered in the same clothes they had worn in the carriage.

A cockerel cried welcome to the morning and Mary lifted her head from the pillow, leaving an imprint of her face upon the fabric. She looked over at Claire, who yawned and stretched herself out of sleep.

'Morning,' Mary said as she dressed.

'Morning,' Claire replied. 'What are the plans for today?'

'I thought we would call upon the Barretts; Reverend Barrett and Lilian's younger sister Anna will hopefully be home.'

'Mary!' Claire squealed.

She looked down. She'd been twisting the fabric of her dress so tightly that she had almost torn it, she must be feeling more anxious than she had realised. Even though she knew that Reginald Ullmann was not in Dundee, he was holding court in Doddingley, she was stirring up a pot which he had firmly put the lid on. He would not take kindly to Mary stirring it up again.

Mary's confidence revived once they had breakfasted and were on their way. Talking to Reverend Barrett would be lovely, he had always been an easy-going man and shown Mary much kindness when she had stayed with them two years earlier. With the benefit of hindsight, she knew the Scotland trip was not so much about advancing her education as getting her out of Mary Jane's way; Mary had reached an age where she was not so malleable to her stepmother's wants and had questioned aspects of her behaviour; the natural answer had been to send Mary away, and she had vowed never to forgive Mary Jane as she packed her valise, left her father at the dock and sailed away. She had hoped to see some sign of regret as the ship left the harbour, but William Godwin had turned his back on her and walked away — back into his new life with no remorse for his daughter or the life she had left behind.

Life at The Cottage had treated her well, and she had bloomed with the Barretts, enjoying the camaraderie of the two sisters and the visits from Adele. In Scotland, she had developed her love of gothic literature and they had spent too many nights reading Ann Radcliffe in hushed voices by candlelight. It was also there that she had her first nightmare of the monster, the shadowy vision that sporadically plagued her dreams when life spiralled out of control. He had been a regular bedfellow during her endless winter. In her nightmares she had walked down the corridor to her crying baby, but the corridor had no end and she sobbed with exhaustion as she walked and walked but never got closer. When she had collapsed against a wall, the baby's crying stopped and relief had dried her tears, only for the source of the baby's silence to be revealed — it was dead and in the arms of the monster. Mary's screams had woken Percy. Mary shook herself out of that memory, dwelling on fictitious monsters was a waste of time when the world held real ones — like Reginald Ullmann. She was determined to prove it.

'Has Dundee always been so blank and dreary?' Claire asked as they walked towards the northern banks of the town.

Mary looked around. True, the skyline wore the black outlines of the docks and chimneys and the cobbled streets shone with a grey tone darker than those in London, but she had never thought of the place as blank. For her, it was full of character and life — a place of hard work and industry and honest people. It felt like home.

'I think of it as the site of my awakening,' Mary replied, hoisting up her skirt to cross a stile. 'Where you see blankness, I see freedom.'

Claire pursed her lips and Mary strode forward, determined not to give audience to Claire's negativity. Living on Piccadilly Terrace had spoiled her and given her a taste of the fine life. Now they were in the wild heart of Scotland, perhaps Claire's own heart would feel able to share its secrets.

'Speaking of freedom, or the lack of it, how is Lord Byron enjoying married life?'

'Byron?' Claire huffed. 'How would I know?'

'We may not have shared a house these past months, Claire, but I do not believe your character is so altered that I cannot read it. There is no way you could live so near to the man who has been the very idol of your romantic aspirations and do nothing.'

'What is there to do when the subject of your affections is a married man?' Claire sighed before realising the stupidity of her words, putting a hand to her mouth.

'I take no offence, Claire.' Mary knew the words were said too quickly to be intended to wound; after all, the facts remained. Percy was a married man when she met him, and he was still a married man. Now she was pregnant with his child. Nothing of his marital status had changed, even if his affections had.

'A marriage contract does not make a man blind to the attentions of others. Especially if the man is a poet with a reputation like Byron's.'

'He cares nothing about his reputation.' Claire sighed, her expression turning to one of affection with a hint of wistfulness about the eyes.

'So, you have met him? You must be familiar with him to know such *intimate* thoughts.'

'We met at a recital Lady Mawdsley held to celebrate the release of "Hebrew Melodies" and —'

'I have not read that, how is it?' Mary interrupted.

'Marvellous. As I was saying, I met him then and again the following morning at Lady Mawdsley's house. I have not seen him since and that is the truth.'

'Right.' Mary nodded. Claire's cheeks flushed, proving to Mary there was more to the story than Claire was admitting; but they had reached the house now and Mary had successfully steered the conversation away from Percy's marital status, which made her walk promptly and proudly as they took the steps up to the house.

Mary knocked at the door. The path to the cottage was decked in beautiful trees whose branches shimmered with orange leaves, the blank streets had given way to curves of scorched yellow; the cottage seemed grander and wider in this autumn sunlight, its eaves and gables sheltering it like curved hands.

'Mary Godwin.' Reverend Barrett's smiling face was like another burst of sunshine. 'How capital to see you! And who is this bonny young woman with you?'

'This is my sister Claire.'

'It is very good to meet you, Claire.' He stretched out his hand and bowed his head. Claire raised her eyebrows at Mary and accepted the hand.

'Come in, come in. You will take tea, won't you? I know it is not the right time, but any time is high tea when good friends arrive.'

Mary smiled. It was such a relief to be greeted in this jovial way, it would make the awkward questions about Reginald easier. Reverend Barrett was such a positive person who was unlikely to spot any ulterior motive in asking them. He would not know that Reginald had been unkind to her and Percy at Adele's wedding and would doubtless just be interested in hearing more about it.

'Do excuse the mess, I'm just trying to make sense of the parish accounts.'

Mary noticed the desk in his study was buckling under the weight of papers and ledgers. She had not realised that being a member of the clergy brought with it such onerous tasks.

'Do you have to do all that alone? Do you not have help with it?'

'There is a parish council, and the landlords are very good at keeping their accounts up to date, but if they do not send their payments, I have to chase them up and as you may remember, Mary, I am not very good at being stern.'

He tried to put on a stern voice and frown, but even the action of it was enough to send Mary and Claire into a fit of giggles. It was true, she could not for a moment imagine him taking on chasing up parish dues and taxes; she could not imagine that anyone would want to put this friendly, caring man in that position.

'Do you have to do this every year?'

'Yes, it is supposed to happen in springtime, but I have been rather distracted this year. Lilian used to be such a help, as did Reginald, but now they have abandoned me to my own accounts everything takes so much longer.' He burst into laughter, smacking his hands on his pantaloons as he spoke. The brightness of his cheeks made his white hair shine bright as the moon.

'I suppose you've found Reginald to be a great help in matters of business.' Claire asked as the reverend passed over the teacup. So much detection was made palatable by the addition of tea, Mary thought.

'Yes, he is an eminent authority on business, having come from a family line of successful merchants.'

Mary listened intently, careful not to give away any expression or detail that might arouse suspicion. As far as Reverend Barrett knew, Mary and Lilian were as close as they had always been, with no Reginald-shaped divide between them.

'I was sorry to hear about Charlotte,' Mary murmured. 'She was such a kind soul.'

'Yes, she was.' With this, the reverend bowed his head and melted into a state of serene sorrow.

'I miss her very much, we all do, and to die in childbirth like that.'

Mary swallowed. To think that both mother and child had made it almost all the way to a successful birth was tragic.

'I am sorry, Mary. I know that you yourself were born under the same unhappy circumstances.'

'I was.' Mary swallowed, hastily putting down the teacup and pulling herself together. Now was not the time to lose her nerve or get distracted by sorrow. The thing about persistent grief was that it was precisely that — persistent. 'It is no wonder Reginald felt the loss so profoundly.'

A small flicker of bitterness creased the reverend's brow. It was so imperceptible that had Mary not been on guard, watching for it, it might have slipped by unnoticed.

'Yes, well, we all did.'

'But Lilian and Reginald growing closer and now on the cusp of their own parenthood.' Claire picked up the conversation. 'That must be thrilling for you.'

He smiled again. 'It is one reason I am trying to sort out the parish affairs before the baby is born. I must be the first to visit!'

'I visited Doddingley for Adele Somerton's wedding in the spring.'

'You did? How charming.' The reverend clasped his hands together in an expression of pure joy. 'You must tell me all about it. Of course, I was invited myself but could not go due to church business keeping me here. I would have loved to have gone; I was always so fond of Adele.'

'Reginald and Lilian have made quite a life down there.'

'Yes.' He hesitated. 'He could not wait to move her away from me and Anna and everyone who loves her.'

There it was again. The sorrow blended with bitterness. Only this time more pronounced.

'Lilian seems happy and well. Though I did not get as much time alone with her as I would have liked.'

'Well, no, you would not. Reginald believes a woman to be the property of the husband, to be danced about like a puppet.' He bit his lip, but tears appeared in his eyes and he swallowed hard. 'I have heard little from her since she moved. The odd letter, but that is all.' Mary was surprised. She had never seen him so out of humour.

'Reassure yourself that Lilian is well and content. The baby will be the making of her and I'm sure there will be more visits here than you will know what to do with.'

Reverend Barrett smiled at Mary's words and wiped at his eyes with his handkerchief.

'I do hope you are right.' He sighed. 'I have lost one daughter to him; I will *not* lose another.'

They took their leave of Reverend Barrett and started the walk back to the inn in silence. For Mary, it was confirmation that Reginald was not favoured by Barrett, which left the question of why had he insisted on their marriage? If he had found Reginald so distasteful, why hadn't he stopped the growing affection between them? What other motive could there be for agreeing to the union?

Claire had become increasingly fidgety as the walk progressed, huffing and puffing, until Mary finally gave in and started a conversation between them.

'Well, Claire, you are as fully conversant with all the facts of the case as myself, what do you think now?'

'I think Reverend Barrett hates Reginald and blames him for the death of his daughter and grandchild, though I did not feel it appropriate to delve further into the details.'

'But how could it be his fault?' Mary countered.

'Did your father not blame the doctor whose infected hands spread the disease that killed your mother? If we were to ask him what killed Mary Wollstonecraft, would he not, even after all these years, still exhibit powerful signs of bitterness, even hatred, at the mention of the doctor?'

Mary shrugged. She had never dared ask about her mother's death; Claire knew far more of it than she did. Obviously, Mary Jane had been much freer with the details of her mother's demise than William Godwin.

'It is not a subject that Father will talk about.' Mary spoke quietly, a sad twist in her stomach reminding her that he had not spoken to her of anything for fourteen months — long enough for two pregnancies, multiple houses, and a lifetime of growing up. He had made it abundantly clear that Mary had severed all ties with the family when she had boarded the boat to Paris with Percy. The baby kicked, bringing her back to the present, reminding her to be happy in it and not wistful about the past. Her future was with Percy.

'Do you think Reginald could have blackmailed Reverend Barrett? That he used Lilian as some sort of collateral?'

'What a ridiculous notion!' Mary huffed. 'How could Reverend Barrett possibly be blackmailed? On what grounds? He did not wear the correct coloured garments for advent? No, that is a preposterous idea.' She walked on, leaving Claire trailing behind.

'Wait a minute,' Claire continued, breathless. 'If the reverend hates Gerald so much, then why stand back and let him marry his daughter, especially if he was convinced that he was responsible for the death of the first?' Claire stopped walking. 'What else can it be?' She waved her arms. 'And what about you?'

'What about me?' Mary turned around.

'Your father refuses to see you yet continues to harass Percy for money for the publishing business. If he hears talk of Percy getting an increase in his allowance or some other financial windfall then he is the first to act on it; but does he talk to you about it or include you in any of the conversations? No!'

Anger flooded Mary's veins. She knew Godwin had asked for money in the past but presumed them to be loans against a publishing deal; she had ignored the previous gossip of the ton that implied he had sold Claire and Mary off to Percy for a thousand pounds, but the thought that he continued to tighten the financial screws on Percy when she had heard nothing from him and he and Mary Jane had actually crossed the street and pretended not to see her when she had encountered them in London, that was too much.

'How do you know he continues to ask Percy for money?' Mary asked.

'My mother tells me in her letters. She tells me everything.'

'Apart from the thousand pounds Percy gave him last summer, what else has he given him?'

'A loan secured against Percy's future inheritance, for a start,' Claire replied.

'Against his future inheritance? So there is to be nothing for his wife or children?' she blurted, the words spilling out before she remembered to correct them. They were a stark reminder that there was a wife and other children that had just as much claim on Percy as she did — perhaps more so. Mary's head was swimming. For her father to take Percy's money but offer nothing to Mary, not even a brief courtesy call to the house, hurt beyond measure. And for Mary Jane to be telling Claire of the information by letter just proved how little her good opinion meant to him now — he who had been everything to her. Mary's mind turned to Reverend Barrett. She wondered just how many of *his* letters had been ignored? How many times the reverend had written to Reginald imploring him to pass the information on to Lilian only for his letters to be tossed into the fire? The conversation with him had proved Mary's instincts to be true — Reginald could not be trusted. They needed to talk to Anna to see if she could shed any light on the situation. But that could wait for later. Now they needed to go back to the inn, have something to eat, and think through everything they had learnt.

CHAPTER THIRTEEN

Anna met them the next morning. She was waiting outside The Cottage and waved at Mary with excitement as they walked up the path.

'I could not wait to see you.' She charged forward, almost knocking Mary to the ground with the weight of her affection. When Mary steadied herself and rubbed her stomach, Anna's eyes swept over it.

'Mary, you are pregnant! I am so sorry — I nearly knocked you down.'

She spoke as if Mary herself was unaware of what had just happened.

'No harm was done and yes, I am with child, just like Lilian.'

'How funny you should both be pregnant at the same time.' Anna smiled, her open features showing traces of both Lilian and their father and inspiring the same joy and affection for Mary.

'It is a coincidence, yes.'

'A most happy one.' Anna clapped her hands together. Two years younger than Lilian, Anna was a romantic soul who believed in the happily-ever-afters of romances and myths — one for whom the real world was the fictional one. Mary had often wished she had the same sensibility; life would be so much easier — and brighter.

She did not know how much more she would learn about Reginald. Whatever he had done, Anna was probably too young to have paid much attention to either his courtship of Charlotte or Lilian, and the chances of her seeing him in any role other than the dashing, sensitive man bereaved too soon before gaining a second chance of love with the second sister, was slim. Still, she would try. Mary took a deep breath and braced herself to ask a most direct question.

'Tell me, Anna, why does your father think Reginald killed Charlotte?'

'Don't be so absurd, Mary, of course Reginald didn't want to kill Charlotte. What a terrible thing to say.'

'I am not saying that he did, just that your father thought he might.' Mary tried to calm Anna down, but she paced around like a directionless chicken. It wasn't an entirely unreasonable response to your brother-in-law being called a murderer.

'Reginald loved Charlotte,' Anna entreated, grasping Mary's hands and looking her in the face with such an earnest expression that Mary felt sorry for having asked the question.

'I do not doubt that he did, but you must admit that his relationship with Lilian moved quickly, and your father does not seem to wholeheartedly endorse it.'

'Reginald wanted a clean break and the chance of a fresh start with Lilian,' Anna replied. 'Is that really so unreasonable?'

Mary thought she had a point. There had been so many times during the past two years when she and Percy had moved from place to place to sidestep uncomfortable memories or hide their tracks from landlords or bailiffs; every single one of those had been heralded as a fresh start when more often than not they had carried the past along with them in each heavy crate.

'Lilian and Reginald grew closer when Charlotte was taken ill,' Anna continued. 'My father could see it happening before they did and was so quick to voice his disapproval at the impropriety of their speed that he actively pushed them together.' She took a deep breath, uncertainty twitching at the corners of her lips.

'And then?'

'And then they married and moved and now we are alone. All because of my father's sense of propriety.'

If the speed of their romance was the reason for their elopement and betrothal, then surely Reginald's judgement on her romance with Percy was doubly harsh and hypocritical. Was he casting scorn on their relationship to assuage his guilt over the origins of his own? Another theory rushed into Mary's mind: perhaps the good people of Doddingley — including Reverend Clarke — knew nothing of the origins of Lilian and Reginald's relationship, only the external display of propriety and respectability their marriage afforded. Keeping Lilian away from anyone who might shatter that illusion might have been the true motive behind Reginald's decision to move to Doddingley.

'How was Reginald with you?' Mary thought a change of subject might make Anna less brittle. 'How was your relationship with him?'

'Entirely as it ought to be. He is much older than me and has long been my brother-in-law. He has been a constant source of support and moral guidance.'

'And do you not look to your father for those qualities?'

Anna snorted. 'Those whose livelihood revolves around providing guidance and support may find their reserves dried up by the time they get home.'

Mary knew exactly what Anna meant.

'I have often thought that about my own father,' she said. 'He writes so eloquently about freedom, liberation and tolerance, and yet he is an angry and impatient man at home, pacing around the place at the slightest upset, complaining at anything that displeases him. Is that not so, Claire?'

'Yes,' replied Claire, 'it is most tiresome. From my part, there has always been Mother to absorb the worst of his tempests, but where there isn't a wife…'

'Where there isn't a wife and his chief advisor has moved to Doddingley…' Anna picked up a flower and began plucking off the petals one by one, throwing it aside once entirely demolished. 'The one remaining daughter is the one to suffer.'

Mary's heart twisted at the icy delivery of the words. A picture of Fanny crept into her mind; her wide-eyed, straightforward sister with none of Claire and Mary's fire or independence, a woman whose life would always be dictated by the rhythms and whims of others.

'Was Reginald so important to your father?'

'Hopelessly so.' Anna sighed. 'It is my view that he allowed Reginald to marry Lilian to keep him here. He was devastated when they left, and…' Anna hesitated, staring at Mary through narrowing eyes which showed that the brief time of their separation had done much to harden Anna's world view and sensibilities; the frivolous girl she'd known before was a thing of the past, and Mary mourned her invisible passing.

'And, Anna?'

'And he allowed Reginald to marry Lilian to prevent our ruin.'

Anna took them into the house and revealed the rest of the story; how her father had always been terrible with paperwork and had relied on their late mother to help keep the parish records in order. Years ago, it had been an easier job, but now that agriculture was booming and law upon law had been brought in that gave the parish more responsibility in collecting and distributing funds, the reverend had found balancing the books an increasingly precarious task. Reginald, with all his business acumen, had kept the family afloat for longer than he should have. Marrying Charlotte and then Lilian had been some sort of reward for his loyalty.

'Now that Lilian is pregnant, I pray that all goes well. I am the final sacrificial lamb and I have no desire to be married to Reginald.' Anna shivered.

'Surely there are others that can help your father with the parish accounts?' Claire said.

'I am sure that there are, the church has networks of people with roles I could not name or fathom, but he would never ask for help and we are sinking.' Anna's shoulders slumped with the sudden weight of her burden. Had the situation been different and Anna been the middle daughter, Lilian's sensible manner and clear head would have proved an excellent addition to the household, there would be no rooms of bourgeoning bills and unpaid taxes in her household. Yet she was promised off and married while Anna — for whom life as the wife of an important man would have been perfect — was here, floundering in a sea of parchment.

'Do you think the reverend will allow us to help him?' Claire asked. 'I have recently joined the ranks of the employed and have some experience in household expenses.'

'I cannot imagine Lady Mawdsley giving you rein of the household purses,' Mary chuckled, picturing Claire balancing one new hat against a new dress — that was her idea of finances.

'These past few months have taught me a good many skills, Mary.' Claire pursed her lips.

A pang of guilt tightened her chest, reminding Mary that she had put Claire in this situation; but the memory of the bonfire swept the guilt aside. She had been entirely justified in her actions, anyone else would have acted in the same way. If she had not sought their separation, then this fresh friendliness between them would never have been possible.

'You have blossomed beyond measure,' Mary replied. Claire smiled, bathing in the glow of Mary's compliment and, mercifully, that was the end of it.

'Would your father accept financial advice?' Mary pressed Anna. 'If not from us, then perhaps from Mr Shelley? There is nothing Percy does not know about debt, consolidation, and promissory notes.'

Anna shook her head. 'Father would be angry with me for even suggesting he cannot cope with the parish responsibilities. He fears they are out to replace him with a younger man and this would be the final nail in the coffin.'

Mary suddenly shot up from her seat, moving at such a speed she banged the table and made the china cups quiver.

'The Doddingley vicar had been about to retire before he was killed,' she declared loudly. If only she had paid more attention to the Reverend Clarke; his role in the wedding had been concluded by the time she and Percy had finally rolled into the village. By the time of the wedding breakfast, his role in the proceedings had been concluded. He was seated somewhere near the bride and groom, on the table between their own and Reginald and Lilian.

'What if —' Mary continued, hoisting a finger into the air — 'what if those hard daggers Percy believed to be thrown at him by Reginald were actually intended for the someone else?'

Claire shook her head. 'I do not think that likely, Mary. Reginald was celebrating the wedding of his best friend, why would he spoil that with anger?'

'Perhaps,' Mary spoke slowly as the possibilities unravelled in her mind, 'he knew that the vicar would soon be murdered and was waiting for it to happen?'

'Do you not think that somewhat fantastical, Mary?' Claire asked.

'I cannot shake my distrust of Reginald.' Mary shrugged. 'I think he is capable of anything.'

'Even murder?'

'Perhaps.'

'I think you are allowing your dislike of him to cloud your judgement.' Claire grabbed her hand. 'Be careful.'

That evening, Mary and Claire were invited to dinner with Anna and Reverend Barrett. Though the table groaned with sumptuous food and claret, Mary found it hard to swallow, knowing as she did the financial strain that lay behind this display of excess. Conversation flowed easily, kept to superficial subjects and the sharing of memories that made Claire quiet and reflective and suddenly more interested in the potatoes than normal. Anna and Mary laughed as they recalled racing the high winds up the hills and thinking that black clouds were shadowy spectres about to raise a stiff hand from heaven and sweep them up. The reverend shook his head at such talk, dismissing it with the straightforward manner of a man firm in his own convictions. Mary tried to bring the conversation around to money but could think of no natural lead, so instead, she turned it to subjects she knew well — poetry and Percy.

'He seems determined to pursue the poetry path, rather than philosophy.'

'Quite right,' the reverend sniffed. 'More money to be made in poetry than philosophy. Will he ever write for Godwin's press?'

Mary shook her head. Her father would accept Percy's words if they were written on a cheque, but not in the form of poetry.

As far as she knew, he had never offered to publish Percy's poetry, which — now she came to think of it — seemed spectacularly ungrateful, given how much Percy had invested in the publishing firm.

'No, Father prefers to publish historical and philosophical treatise. Percy has many ideas, but no specific theory.'

She quickly forked food into her mouth, hopeful that Reverend Barrett would not ask further questions on Percy's philosophy or morality. He clearly knew that Percy and Mary lived as a couple, there was no way of concealing the curve of her stomach or the baby gaining strength beneath it, but she was tired of having to explain or justify herself. All she wanted now was food, sleep and the truth.

'I do enjoy poetry.' The reverend chewed enthusiastically as he spoke. 'I am especially fond of Byron.'

'Claire has met Lord Byron,' Mary said, a wicked smile appearing on her face; Claire kicked her leg under the table.

'Really? What is he like?' Barrett's eyes widened, and he shovelled another large fork full of potatoes into his mouth as he waited for Claire's answer.

'He is everything you would expect him to be,' Claire said, evenly. Mary was impressed. She'd said it without a sigh or a swoon. 'A genius, an absolute genius.'

'Claire has been to one of his recitals.'

The reverend shook his head, his cheeks suddenly flushed as he swung his gaze between Anna, Claire and Mary.

'Oh, my dear, that must have been thrilling! Anna, imagine a recital of Lord Byron's poetry by the man himself.'

'Was it, Claire?' Mary mocked, unable to stop herself. 'Was it thrilling?'

'No one reads his words as well as he does.' Claire attempted to smile meekly, but Mary saw the flicker of higher emotion building beneath it. There was no denying it, Claire was in love. Mary only hoped that Byron at least had the courtesy to let Claire down gently once her moment in the spotlight had passed.

'Perhaps you might call upon Byron to pay a visit here?' Mary was pushing her luck now, but the talk of Byron had loosened Reverend Barrett's reserve, which might make her next step easier.

'Could you, Claire?' Anna leant forward eagerly. Mary knew Claire would never willingly bring such temptation to Byron, she was far too jealous for that.

'I will try.' Claire smiled. Mary knew she would not.

'I was thinking,' Mary said brightly, as if it were something she had just thought about, 'of taking a trip to Doddingley, to visit Lilian and Reginald before the child is born. It must be so boring for Lilian being in confinement, I am sure a visit from you and Anna would be most welcome to her.'

'Oh yes, Father, please let's go! You were saying yourself how you wished we could have gone to Adele's wedding.'

'The church is very busy in springtime, there are rents to be collected, parish taxes to be paid, it was impossible,' Barrett grumbled, the excuses rolling from his tongue in a tired, well-rehearsed manner. 'It was impossible.'

'I know, but that time has passed, harvest has passed, is it not a quieter time until advent?'

'You know the church's calendar more thoroughly than I do, Anna.' He laughed, looking at his daughter with a warm smile that made Mary believe everything might go as planned.

'Our carriage comes tomorrow; we should arrive in Doddingley on Sunday.'

Anna smiled. 'Just in time for church.'

CHAPTER FOURTEEN

'Are we there yet?'

Anna wriggled in the seat next to her father. A chaise without windows had been sent, which had stiffened the air and stifled the atmosphere inside the coach. Mary's nausea had returned, and the only way she could calm it was by closing her eyes and conjuring images of the countryside they passed. On the outskirts of Dundee the sea vapour surrounding the new industrial world of the docks crept into the carriage like fog. Once the industrial smells had subsided, the autumn air gave prominence to woods and forests and Mary pictured the slow, hazy movement of a world turning from golds and greens to grey and white.

Claire had sat quietly reading her small leather volume of Byron's poems, placing the book to her chest when she thought the other members of the carriage were not looking. Percy would love to meet Byron — perhaps once Claire was back in London and they were safely back in the bosom of Windsor, they might bring these poets together. It was good to see Claire's attentions diverted from Percy; there had been a time when Mary feared she may lose Percy to Claire when she had been so wrapped up in grief that she was impenetrable.

They had stopped at two taverns: the reverend crossing himself before entering either venue but vigorously enjoying the revelry and hospitality once inside them. Mary grimaced at the bills they were accruing but was thankful that Percy's financial entanglements with his grandfather had finally been sorted, giving them a financial freedom they hadn't had in a long time. Sometimes, she reminded herself, you just had to live and to hell with the consequences. Mary wouldn't allow herself to go as far as thinking that perhaps their life together was an on upward trend, but secretly she prayed it was. If only they had met without the complicated bonds of Harriet and the children, their life together would have been perfect.

Church bells punctured the air, reminding those who would listen that it was Sunday and time to go to church. They must be in Doddingley now. Mary had not taken the trouble of securing lodgings, hoping that Adele and Donald would house her and Claire, and Lilian and Reginald would- feel dutybound to take Anna and Reverend Barrett. If these plans did not come off, there was always the tavern she and Percy had stayed in previously. Mary's thoughts were disturbed by the sharp pounding on the door which opened, the sharp smell of sweat emanating from the driver reminding her they all needed to freshen up.

'Right, you're here. Where shall I put the luggage?'

'Take them up to the big house on the hill,' Mary said, pointing out Lilian and Reginald's house that bullied the landscape, leaving all the other houses and cottages cowering in its wake. 'Lilian will not go to church if she is in confinement, will she?' Mary blushed, knowing that her own pregnancy and former childbearing should make her the best placed to answer her own question, but she had been chasing grave-robbers around London when others would rest in bed.

'Reginald will be too scared of history repeating itself to take any chances,' Anna said quietly, making all of their thoughts rush back to the tragedy of Charlotte and the baby's earlier deaths.

'Yes, Lilian will be at home.' Reverend Barrett's voice was determined. If Lilian was at the church, his relaxed manner might be easily moved to anger.

'You are expecting me to take all of them up there?' the driver interrupted, his face creased with exasperation. Having dropped them at the destination, he clearly wanted to start the journey back.

'Yes, please. Thank you.' Mary nodded. She watched as the congregation filed through the graveyard and wound their way across the question mark of land that lead to the church. All the residents were there — Mrs Harris, who'd told her that Reginald had swindled her husband out of the Big House, the old man who'd thrown a pale of slop over Reginald — all these people who knew him and tolerated him but kept the secrets of their community like closely guarded jewels. She half expected to see the figure of the chimney sweep loitering in the graveyard, an unwelcome ghoul. She was still convinced he'd been at the graveside, even if Percy thought she was seeing things. Mary thought of Lilian's letter, the panic that raced across the page, her fear that the community wished her ill, that something would happen to her. Percy had put that down to pregnancy and, as Mary's own pregnancy had been plagued by dreams of monsters and shadows, she'd accepted his more rational explanation for that, too. Now, being back in Doddingley, she couldn't shake the feeling that something was about to happen. The sky knew it too, a patch of grey slid across the sun like a curtain; in a few moments, the heavens would open. Mary shivered, realising that everyone was watching her. She composed herself quickly, taking Claire's arm as they walked towards the church and took their place in the congregation.

As Mary shuffled into a pew at the back of the church, she spied Reginald and an icy fear crept over her. He was seated in the front pew with Donald and a couple of the other men from the village. All the important people, set up like bottles in a row. Adele was in the row behind them, flanked by other women, with whom she seemed to exchange bland pleasantries before turning her eyes towards the front of the church. An organ blasted into life and the congregation turned their heads to the sight of the large gold cross that started the procession; its jewelled eyes sending specks of orange, red and golden light onto the path in front of them, gemstones lighting the way to God. A new vicar, a younger one than either Reverend Clarke or the man who'd taken his funeral, smiled and nodded as he walked down the aisle in his green chasuble.

The service began and, standing, the congregation enthusiastically belted out the hymns. Mary could not bring herself to sing. Not because she was a committed atheist, like Percy, but because she was watching the people — still strangers, even though she had met them before — act out the scenes of their own devotion. William Godwin, like Percy, had not foisted religion upon them and apart from a couple of services she'd been to over the years, Mary had never successfully evaluated her own position on religion, independent of those surrounding her. Looking at the depiction of the figure on the cross or the stern saintly faces passing judgement through stained-glass panels, she did not know what she believed. All she was sure of was there was more to the murder of Reverend Clarke than the people of Doddingley were willing to admit. Casting the chimney sweep as the culprit and finding him dead days later had concluded the crime for the villagers, but Mary still was not satisfied and being back in Doddingley brought those feelings of unease back to the surface.

The wooden pews creaked as the congregation sat back down and the sermon began. Mary looked at Reverend Barrett, who was watching the young vicar with interest, his arms folded, a wide smile punctuated by vigorous nods of the head whenever he said something he agreed with. Mary wondered if he knew he was actually grunting, certainly the congregation became increasingly aware of it as faces turned back towards them. Mary could not tell if the thin-lipped expressions were for the vicar or for her.

Reverend Barrett eventually took the hint, putting his hand up in apology and sinking down a little further into the pew like a naughty schoolboy. The service continued with the congregation jumping up in the pews with stoical devotion for the hymns and sitting in serene silence for the dedications and devotions. Claire took the whole ceremony far more seriously than Mary, who watched in faint bemusement at Claire, gripping her hands tightly together in prayer and crossing herself as she sat back up again. It suited her devotion; perhaps once she'd finished with Byron, she could become a nun. Mary guffawed at the thought, attracting a few frowns before turning it into a polite cough. Such a person of contradictions. claire had always been more enigmatic than she. Mary was an open book, a quiet, frequently dull — to her mind — book, but she was glad of the simplicity of her emotions.

Eventually, the congregation was called forward to join in the communion. Reverend Barrett nudged Anna into action, and Claire got up from the pew and gestured for Mary to accompany them. Mary shook her head. It would be hypocritical to accept the body and blood if she didn't believe in it, no matter how hungry she was. Besides, the communion line was long, a visual reminder of the hierarchy of the members of the congregation. The vicar and the altar boy worked quickly and quietly to get the cup and bread together, the altar boy a picture of cherubic concentration as he held the communion vessels to be blessed. A shard of light cut through the stained-glass window, slashing his hand with a stripe of red like a wound, and Mary could see the tremor of the effort of holding the cup up racing through the boy's body. A small church, like a small community, could not keep everything hidden.

Finally, the communion was ready. Mary took advantage of being the only person who hadn't queued up for communion to change her position, moving slowly around the backs of the congregation and positioning herself to the left of the altar, in an alcove which housed a marble statue of a fallen hero. She blessed herself, unsure if she was even doing that right, and nodded towards the statue, paying her respects, and watched as the first row shifted themselves into the space made by the other members of the congregation. Reginald held back, letting Donald go in front of him. The two men paused at the end of the pew. Mary frowned, from this angle it seemed as though both were unwilling to take the first step. After a moment, Reginald nodded and turned to walk towards the altar, as if accepting that this should be the order of things. Mary scrambled in her bag to extract her notebook, making a note of it.

Reginald's face seems to suggest that this should be the order of things, she wrote, tapping the pencil against her lip. *This should be the order of things*. What did it mean? Her experiences in detection had given her a good eye for detail and the confidence to trust and follow her instincts, and something was telling her that Donald and Reginald were both reluctant to be the first to go for communion. Was it part of some deeper problem between them? Had something happened to change their relationship? They had seemed so close at the wedding and had worked solidly together to bring the community to order after the murder of the vicar.

175

The vicar opened his arms and welcomed the congregation to the altar, encouraging them to kneel in a line. Donald and Reginald took their place at the altar, and though their heads were bowed, their knuckles were as white as the marble floor. Melodious words were sung into the air as the communion cup was passed first to Donald, then to Reginald. Once Donald had taken his sip, he seemed to stretch back and smile at Reginald. Reginald kept his gaze forward.

A sudden wave of terror passed over Mary, but she didn't know why. *This should be the order of things.* She slid out of the pew and down the side of the church to the lady chapel that ran alongside the altar, better for a good view of the two men. Reginald was shaking. For a moment, Mary's vision was impaired by the altar boy, preparing the second part of the communion and obscuring her view of Reginald taking the wine. Suddenly there was a tremendous crash and Mary's brain scrambled to make sense of the scene before her.

Reginald and Donald's bodies lay motionless on the floor, the wine from the broken chalice running into the stone crevices around them.

Screams pierced the air and the flock buzzed around in hysterical confusion. The vicar's face blanched and the altar boy bolted from the scene, his hand clamped over his mouth; the sound of his retching echoing through the open door.

'What *is* happening?' Reverend Barrett barged his way to the front, arriving at the altar at the same time as Claire and Anna.

Anna spied the body of her brother-in-law and put her hand to her mouth, her eyes welling with tears.

'Quick, check their pulses!' Barrett spurred them into action.

'H-how do I do that?' Anna stammered.

'Like this.' Claire knelt down and grabbed Donald's wrist, feeling the soft part of the flesh where the veins were blue. 'He's still alive,' she sighed, detecting a pulse.

Together, Claire and Mary turned Reginald onto his back. They gasped in horror at the sight of his protruding eyes and blue lips.

'There's no pulse,' said Claire, taking his wrist. 'There's nothing there.'

'Let me see.' Barrett pushed the members of the congregation — who were busy calling for a doctor and smelling salts — aside. He clutched at his chest.

'He's dead!' he cried.

CHAPTER FIFTEEN

'Get out of my way. I must check the body.' Dr Snelling spoke quickly, his hands moving over the body checking the pulse, opening the mouth, the eyes as if Reginald might be resuscitated by the activity. They moved into place, positioning themselves behind the bodies and lifting them up. Mary and the rest of her group looked on with stunned faces.

'Why is it that *everywhere* you go, murder follows?' Claire whispered to Mary. Mary nudged Claire in the ribs, but her comment had been overheard by Dr Snelling, whose eyes narrowed in stony disapproval.

'I bet they still have the ducking stool here,' Claire continued, oblivious.

'Claire!' Mary turned to her sharply. 'If you cannot be productive, then please stop trying to be humorous.'

Mary turned her gaze back to the scene. The bodies had been propped up against the altar bars like sleeping drunks. Reginald's body was covered with a black sheet. There was nothing to be done for him.

'Lilian!' Reverend Barrett suddenly barked, shaking his head as if waking from a nightmare. 'We must tell Lilian.'

Mary put an arm around him. 'Perhaps it is best for you and Anna to see her first, the blow of such horrendous news will be softened by your kindness.'

Anna escorted her father out of the church, their murmurs of disbelief echoing up through the church's draughty vaults and back across the pews before the wooden door slammed shut behind them.

'Who prepared the bread and wine?' Mary asked.

The vicar froze, locked into his position at Donald's shoulders, hoisting him up. Why was he doing that? Did he think he had choked and the position would help dislodge some unknown obstruction?

'It is kept in the vestry, then brought to the altar before the service begins.'

'And who put it there today? You?'

The vicar shook his head. 'No, not me. Perhaps it was Charles?' He turned to the pale altar boy, who had staggered back into the church, wiping his mouth. 'Charles, did you prepare the Eucharist for today's service?'

Charles shook his head. 'No, sir, it was already prepared when I put on my robes. I brought it up to the altar, that's all.'

He looked at the bodies again. The colour that had only just returned to his cheeks exited sharply as he clamped his hand to his mouth and ran back down the aisle. Mary watched him go. Her chest tightened at the idea of this young boy taking the blame for someone else's crime. One look at his ashen face was enough to know that he was not guilty.

Her thoughts were interrupted by the doctor. 'Quickly, the smelling salts! He's coming round.'

Adele — who Mary had quite forgotten in all this commotion — burst into tears and rushed towards her husband, stumbling in her haste to reach him.

'Oh, Donald, thank goodness!'

Donald put his hand to his forehead, accepting Adele's arm as he stirred back into consciousness. Had he encountered the same distant blackout as before? That reminded her, she was still awaiting a letter from James Berry.

'What happened?' His voice was thick and drowsy, like one who'd just awoken from sleep.

'I don't know,' Adele stammered. 'You and Reginald collapsed. You ... you... Oh, Donald.' She sobbed on his shoulder. Donald stretched out a hand towards her.

'What has happened? Where is Reginald? My throat burns. Has someone meant to poison us all?'

He was right. If all the congregation had come to the altar, then the entire village would have suffered the same fate. Mary's mind raced back to Paris and to Monsieur Lamont's attempts to poison his wife. She recognised the signs of poisoning from the descriptions she'd given and the long conversations she'd had with James Berry on the best way to dispose of a body. Mary sighed. She could really use his wisdom now.

The chorus of coughs from Donald broke through Mary's thoughts, reminding her that two had been poisoned, but only one had died.

'Claire, can you check on the altar boy outside, make sure he is revived?'

Claire nodded, lifted her skirts, and raced down the aisle, the fabric rustling as she moved.

'Donald needs to go home,' said the doctor. 'I will give him a diuretic to clear his system, that will expel the toxins.'

'But do you not worry that someone poisoned the Eucharist? That the act was intended for all of you?'

The doctor towered over her, bringing his face to hers. Mary stiffened.

'I heard what your friend said to you, that every time you come to Doddingley, it ends in murder. I would be very careful about throwing accusations around. You might find they stick on you.'

Mary's heart pounded. Was that a threat? A sensible person might turn on their heels and run away as fast as they could, but Mary had always been up for a fight, especially when the truth was at stake.

The screams that pierced the air as Mary and Claire arrived at the Big House confirmed Lilian had been told the news. Mary thought of the baby, that fragile cargo — how would it cope with the physical reactions of Lilian's body? What if the shudders that accompanied her screams were enough to dislodge it from its safe haven? Mary's own mind flew back to her own grief and Clara, bursting open the wound afresh. A gentle flutter from her stomach reminded her of the new life within it, the possibility of hope after sorrow.

Mary and Claire followed the path to the door and opened it carefully. The screaming had been replaced by sobs that cloaked the house in sorrow. Lilian was bookended by her family; the reverend sat with his arm around her shoulders, holding her up, while Anna held her hand on the other side. Although the depth of her sorrow broke Mary's heart, she felt comforted that Lilian had the people who loved her the most when she needed them.

'Mary!' Lilian's voice still held a scrap of surprise. Mary rushed over to her, kneeling in front of her and taking Lilian's hands in hers.

'Lilian. I am so sorry.'

'I cannot believe it; it does not seem real.' Lilian took a deep breath. 'I cannot fathom what is happening in Doddingley. It used to be such a safe place, full of kind people. Now, it is nothing but a poison to me.'

Mary gulped. It was an unfortunate choice of words given the circumstances of Reginald's death. But even in her outward show of sympathy, questions buzzed around her head and would not be silenced. If the door to the church was left open before the service, then anyone from the village could have taken the opportunity to lace the communion cup with poison. But who had the motive? Whoever it was had banked on two things: first, that Reginald would go to church and second, that the Farmer's Council would take communion before the other residents. Mary's stomach suddenly gave a loud rumble. They had travelled for a long time, and she was tired and hungry.

'I have called for tea and refreshments,' Lilian sniffed, dabbing at her eyes with her handkerchief. Mary blushed. Even in her darkest moments Lilian did not escape her social conventions.

'That is so very kind, Lilian,' Claire replied. Mary was glad of the diversion of attention away from her body's mumblings.

'Will you stay here?' Lilian's voice shook. 'Will you stay until after the funeral?'

Mary bit her lip. She had only intended to stay for a couple of days to ensure that all was well; she had not expected murder to follow in their tracks. There would be no way of keeping this quiet from Percy if they stayed until after the funeral, which would come after a post-mortem and inquest, and there was no way of knowing how long such proceedings would take; but when she looked at her friend's face and saw the deep sorrow freshly etched into her eyes and knew of the anguish of the days and the weeks to come, there was no other place for her.

'Of course we will.'

'Mary, a word outside, please.' Claire nodded towards the door and Mary followed. Once they were out of earshot, Claire turned to Mary.

'I cannot stay here indefinitely. Lady Mawdsley will return imminently, and if I am not there when she does, I will lose my position.'

'But surely she would sympathise if you sent news of the situation?'

'No, she would not.' Claire shook her head. 'I do not know Lilian, nor her family. I joined in this adventure to renew our friendship. You are needed here, but I am not.'

'It would have nothing to do with the return of a certain dashing poet, would it?'

'Lady Byron is near her own confinement. His scant attentions will fall on her, not me.'

'Are you so fond of being a paid companion you rush back to it?' Mary's voice trembled. She had got used to Claire being around again and was in no rush to send her away. But it was much easier to say that with Percy out of the picture. Who knew if old rivalries and jealousies would rear their heads once all three were reunited?

'I can go to Windsor and tell Percy what has happened?'

'I can do that by post.'

'I can get there quicker.' Claire sighed. 'I did not want to bring this up, but I fear it is the only thing that will make you understand.'

A sense of trepidation rose in Mary's stomach. What on earth was she going to say?

'I am not good with death,' Claire began. 'I reacted horribly to Clara's death. I did not know how to react; all I could think about was moving on and getting back to how things had been before.' Claire spoke quickly, scarcely stopping for breath.

'Is that why you burned her clothes?'

Claire nodded. 'You had both been so altered by the loss. You in particular, Mary, were unrecognisable. Percy retreated into poetry, but it was dark and horrible, with none of his usual beauty at all. And I could see you drifting apart from each

183

other.' Claire's voice broke, tears fell down her cheeks. 'I wanted to bring you back together.'

'That is why you destroyed everything? Not because you were jealous that we had been away?'

'I could never offer Percy the comfort you bring. I could not even try to. I am no substitute for you. But it wasn't Percy I grieved for, Mary, it was you.'

Mary's heart swelled and tears pricked at her own eyes. Was she hearing things? Had Claire just admitted that it was Mary she had missed? Mary she was trying to resurrect from her grief? Not Percy's affection, whatever that had meant. If that was true — and the emotions pouring out of Claire suggested it was — then everything Mary had feared about having Claire around lessened. It would never completely evaporate, because she could not shake the notion that they had been intimate.

'Come back to Windsor with us, live with us again.' The words left Mary's mouth before she was even convinced that she meant them. Claire's eyes shone, and a smile danced across her lips.

'That is very kind, Mary, but no, I do not want to live with you again. I will visit, if I may? I enjoy being a companion, it gives me a sense of purpose.'

'Even if you are a companion to an ogre?'

'Lady Mawdsley is not so bad.' Claire smiled. 'Her bark is most certainly worse than her bite, rather like Persephone. I will get a carriage back from the inn. I will stay there tonight. I will just collect my things.'

'Are you sure?' Mary replied, her face creasing into a frown. She wasn't used to this side of Claire. She was changing, maturing, and all for the better.

'Yes, I am more useful to Lady Mawdsley now. Be with your friend. We did not expect, when we set off on this adventure, to be facing another murder. Did we?'

'No,' Mary agreed. 'I was rather hoping to bring the first one to a satisfactory conclusion, but now...' She hesitated. The links between the crimes would not come, no matter how she coaxed them. 'Now my primary care is looking after Lilian.'

Lilian, whose sobs had travelled through the open door and directly into Mary's heart, increased her determination to look after her. With the reverend and Anna, they would make sure Lilian was well looked after and comforted in her grief, shielding her from further harm and keeping her unborn child as safe as they could. Companionship, care and conversation were the remedies she needed now.

'I suppose I shall have to let people know.' Lilian sighed, her gaze falling upon Mary and Claire as they re-entered the room.

'We can do that,' her father replied, patting her hand in a soothing manner. 'Do not concern yourself with such things.'

'An organised man like Reginald must have an address book?' Anna said.

The talk of letters pricked something in Mary's mind. She remembered the letters that Lilian had written, those pleading missives that had brought her here. In all the hustle and bustle of the morning's events, she had quite forgotten them. Now she had brought her mind back to them she could think of nothing else and as she sat back down and listened to the conversation happening around her, Mary found it difficult to reconcile the noble, calm woman who sat before her with the hysterical, paranoid woman of the letters — a woman who was fearful for her life and that of her unborn child. Whom had she thought of as such a threat? Who amongst their small community had brought Lilian to the point of desperation that made her write to Mary for help? Mary was suddenly itching to find out, but it wasn't the time or place. Asking such questions would rightly lead to Mary being asked to leave by Reverend Barrett and alienate Lilian from her affections forever when she had only just got her back in her life. She would just have to wait until the first clouds of grief had passed and perhaps then she could bring the letters up.

CHAPTER SIXTEEN

'It's so good of you to call.' Adele's voice comprised its usual sweetness, but her manner seemed a little more distracted than usual. It was to be expected in the circumstances. She hurried around the room, moving objects and tidying surfaces, only her abrupt tone towards the housekeeper gave any indication of the stress she must be harbouring under the surface.

'I am staying with Lilian for a while,' Mary replied, shaking her head at the invitation to tea.

'How is she bearing up?' Adele sat down, but even this action was accompanied by the restless tapping of feet. It was as if she just couldn't stay still. Mary wondered what was causing such restlessness.

'She is devastated, as you would expect.'

'Such a tragedy.' Adele shook her head, but her eyes fell away, taking her attention with it. Something was definitely on her mind, Mary hoped she would discover what it was.

'And Donald, how is he?'

Adele hesitated. Her brow furrowed and for a moment she looked as though she were in pain. 'He is much restored,' she said after a moment's reflection that seemed to Mary too unnaturally long to be sincere. 'Thank goodness.'

'Is he here now?' Mary asked. She tried to keep her voice as light and even as Adele's had been, but her friend knew her well enough to understand her true meaning. Almost a week had passed since the attempt on his life; Mary thought she had done well to avoid coming here and questioning Donald. He was the only person who could talk Mary through all that had happened at the church. A sudden tightness gripped her —

what if Donald had noticed her hiding in the lady chapel? Would he think it strange that she had been so keen to get to the altar and watch the Eucharist? Her explanation of trying to watch Reginald would only reveal her true suspicions of them. Reginald's death had absolved him of any wrongdoing, even Mrs Harris had mourned his passing when Mary had seen her on her walk around the village. Death had exalted Reginald to a higher position than he had attained in life. Tarnishing his name again would do nothing to further her cause. Even if he were guilty of the earlier deaths, there was no way he had intended his own.

'Is there any word on Reginald's funeral? Has a date been set?'

Mary shook her head. 'No, nothing yet. Lilian is awaiting the results of the post-mortem.'

'Dr Snelling is a man to take his time,' Adele replied. 'Though surely there is nothing to conclude but poisoning?'

Adele had opened the door that Mary was reluctant to, but now it was opened, Mary was keen to see where it would lead.

'I agree, it must be. But who would want to poison Reginald or the rest of the council?' *Best not to single Donald out*, Mary thought. *Adele might be more likely open up if she thought she was being objective.*

Adele shrugged. 'Men of money make as many enemies as friends. This community has not been the same since the death of Reverend Clarke. It's as if a darkness has infected the entire village.' Her voice trembled.

'Infected?' Mary shifted in her seat. Her hands itched to make notes, but she would just have to remember everything Adele said. Her words were not those to be expected from a newlywed. Neither was this grey and heavy expression that masked her beautiful features.

'Has something happened?' Mary sat forward, reaching for Adele's hand. All efforts at eye contact were evaded, and tears shone in Adele's eyes. She bit her lip and shook her head. 'Adele, has something happened to you?'

'I thought I heard voices.'

Adele suddenly sprang up as Donald appeared at the door. He looked paler and thinner, Mary thought, but there were no other visible effects of the poisoning.

'Mary, how lovely to see you!'

He embraced her in an unexpected hug, to which she responded stiffly, before turning his attention to Adele, slipping an arm around her shoulder and pulling her to him. Adele's body seemed as rigid and reluctant as her own, and she turned her face away from him. She caught Mary's eye for the briefest of moments and Mary saw something flash in them, a hesitation, cold and dark. A warning.

'I came to inquire about your health, but I see there was no need, you look very well.'

'Yes, thankfully.' Donald's smile quickly evaporated. 'Terrible business. I still cannot believe Reginald is gone.'

'Yes, quite, quite horrible.'

'Isn't it nice of Mary to come and see you?' Adele's voice resumed its bright, cheery tone. She prodded at her husband's chest with a mocking finger. 'But you should be resting.'

'I am bored with seeing the same walls. I do not know how women can stand to be confined.' Donald nodded towards Mary's stomach. 'You will head for confinement soon yourself.'

Mary shook her head. 'I do not believe in such things. I think it is far healthier for mother and baby to keep going and anyway, I have months to go yet.'

'Months?' Donald raised an eyebrow. 'Then that is a boy you are carrying.'

Mary's heart swelled, rushing a warm sensation through her body. Secretly, that had been her own feeling; how funny Donald should share them. This pregnancy felt different, she was sure that she was holding a placid, even-tempered poet in there — just like his father. How long would it be until Percy got here? Claire had left days earlier, surely, she had got the message to him by now? Her baby — their baby — kicked, reminding her she was never alone. Mary delicately placed her hand over it.

'I have not dared visit Lilian yet.' Adele's words broke through her reverie. 'It seems unjust that I should keep my husband and she should lose hers.'

'But it is not your fault.' Mary put her hand on her friend's shoulder. 'Come back to the house with me, perhaps that will make it easier for you?'

'That sounds like a capital idea,' Donald replied. 'I have my house calls to conduct, and it will be so much easier if you are not here to scold me.' He chuckled. Adele's face broke into a grin and there was a glimmer of the light-heartedness they'd shown at their wedding.

'Well, it is agreed. Are you ready to leave now?' Mary put on her gloves and readied herself to leave. Adele stared at her with wide eyes.

'Now? I cannot leave the house in this dress.'

Mary, who had paid no attention at all to Adele's dress, now stared at it. There was nothing wrong with it as far as she could see. It was a cornflower blue morning dress with a simple empire neckline and a delicate embroidery of flowers at its hem — the perfect dress to bring a little spring magic to a quickly turning season.

'It is a beautiful dress.'

'Beautiful it may be, suitable for visiting a widow it most certainly is not.' Adele laughed, brushing her hand on Mary's shoulder as she walked past. Mary blushed at her unworldliness. She would never give a moment's thought to the appropriateness of her dress. Most of the dresses she owned were in brown or black. All were suitable for mourning. At least that was something.

Now Adele had left the room, she found herself alone with Donald. The air had shifted, the amiable mood of moments earlier replaced by an awkward silence that hung heavily between them like a cloud.

'You may as well sit down again; you are going to have a long wait.'

'Do not feel compelled to stay on my account if you have somewhere else to go.'

Donald stared at her. 'I would not dream of leaving a guest alone. Certainly not one we call a friend.'

Something in the way he said the word friend made Mary shudder. She did not realise it had been so obvious until he asked her if she was cold.

'I have never been very good at dressing for the seasons. I am always too hot in the summer and too cold in the winter. I never seem to get it right.'

'Perhaps Adele can guide you. She has an exceptional talent for choosing the right clothes for each event.'

'She was always very artistic.' Perhaps choosing her outfits was the only artistic freedom Adele had nowadays? Marriage to a man like Donald would surely bring plenty of social events and expectations and conditions with it. She was blessed to have a man like Percy who respected her talents and allowed her the freedom to develop and express them. It was so far from society's ideals.

Conversation retreated and silence descended once more, cloying at Mary's throat. Without the safety of Adele, she did not feel that she could ask Donald the questions she was desperate to ask. She could sense his appraising eyes upon her, as if she were nothing more than a scientific specimen to be dissected and discovered.

'I am ready now, Mary.'

Mary's shoulders lifted and she let out the long breath she hadn't realised she'd been holding. Turning to face Adele, she could not help but examine this new outfit; a black dress in a rich fabric swathed by a respectable coat and fur muffler. Adele looked older and more serious in it, which made Mary's heart pang for the youthful woman in the cornflower blue. She could see how it might be a better choice and wondered if she were the only woman in the world who did not give mind to such concerns.

'Donald, it is good to see you so well. Perhaps I may call on you again? I have a few questions I would like to ask you.'

Mary held out her hand. Donald shook it.

'I have no doubt you do, Mary. Of course. Perhaps you will come to dinner?'

'Oh yes, that would be delightful,' cried Adele. 'Do you think Lilian and her family will come too?'

'It might be too soon for Lilian,' replied Mary, 'but I am sure the Reverend Barrett and Anna would be only too delighted. You can ask them when we get there.'

'Capital!' Adele smiled.

Adele kissed her husband on the cheek, and they bid their farewells. Mary could not shake the feeling that Donald was watching her with something of a suspicious eye. There was something in his manner that unnerved her. The desire to get out her notebook and jot down some things Adele had said was strong, she would have to make some excuse to leave the room once they arrived at Lilian's house before the words were lost forever. The early morning fog had lifted but the frigid chill fermented the air, bringing with it the smells of a decaying autumn slowly mulching into winter. Watching the leaves dart from the trees and the birds take to the skies made her wish that winter would hurry and take the golden jewels of autumn quickly. It was cruel to watch it dying so. Death should be nothing but a moment.

Something in her mind clicked. Pieces of the puzzle started coming together. Mary's heart raced, but she calmed herself down, she would have to take her time.

Mary waited until they were out of the house and halfway down the hill before asking the question that had been bothering her since Adele had talked of the village's darkness; she had heard those words before but had only just recalled where.

'Adele, why did you write to me and pretend to be Lilian?'

'Me? Pretend to be Lilian? Don't be absurd!'

'You wrote to me and signed the letters in her name. You cannot deny it, you've used exactly the same phrases in our conversation today.'

'I do not know what you are talking about, Mary.' Adele stopped walking; her face hardened. 'Lilian must have written them.'

'Lilian never wrote to me. Reginald wouldn't let her. I should have sensed there was something wrong when I received them, but I hoped it was a sign he had changed his mind about me.'

'Well, I do not know who wrote them, but it was not me.' Adele stormed ahead, Mary broke into a jog to keep pace but a stitch in her stomach reminded her of the delicacy of her condition and she stopped to catch her breath. Adele turned around.

'Have you actually asked Lilian about the letters?' she said.

'No, I haven't,' Mary replied, wincing as the sharp pain took hold. Her body doubled over to meet it. She exhaled sharply, hoping it would take the pain away. When it didn't, she rubbed at her stomach, reciting a silent prayer as she did so.

'Mary!' Adele rushed back to her, guiding her by the shoulders towards a small hillock. 'Sit here.'

'It's wet.'

'That doesn't matter.' Adele's voice was firm and her eyes steely. 'All this detecting cannot be good for you or the baby. You must desist.'

Mary slumped down and sighed. Adele was right. It had brought with it as much heartache as reward, and Percy frequently told her off for overdoing things. When they had no money and nothing to do with their time, detecting seemed like an enjoyable way to pass the time, but this time she could not take the chance of anything happening to the baby; her heart would not stand another loss.

'I know you are right, and I will look after myself,' Mary began, 'but you yourself admitted that some sort of darkness has infected the village. Those are your own words, Adele. Surely you cannot be willing to accept that someone tried to kill your husband without wanting answers?'

'It is as I said.' Adele shrugged. 'Men who make money make enemies and you already know that Donald and Reginald own most of the village and that their methods have not always been honourable.'

'And you are not troubled by that? Being married to a man whom others might wish dead?'

'You are not telling me that Mr Shelley has not his own fair share of enemies? I suspect he has an equal share of enemies to admirers.'

Mary thought of the moneylenders and the long autumn nights when Percy drifted in and out of her life like a half-imagined phantom. All that scurrying from dark corner to dark corner, dodging the moneylenders and the bailiffs. She shuddered at the memory.

Adele nodded. 'I see it is not so far from your experience.'

'I feel much better now, we can continue,' Mary said, raising herself up from the ground.

'If you feel certain,' Adele replied, her eyes narrowed with concern.

They walked on in silence, Mary's mind turning over everything Adele had said. It was true that she liked to keep active, and she was realising just how different to other women she was. Many were content to stew in society's standards and desired nothing more than conformity. That was anathema to her. She could just as easily be turned to stone as live a life like that. Her mind was like a nest of hungry birds, always full of sounds and activity, constantly striving for attention and wanting to be nurtured. To starve her mind would be worse than starving her body. There was a time when she had thought Adele to be the same.

'Will you go in first? Make sure I am welcome?' Adele asked.

'Of course you will be welcome, what makes you think you will not?'

'Both men were poisoned, but my husband survived.' Adele spoke quietly. Mary understood the sadness behind her words, and the guilt. 'I had never thought Doddingley to be a dangerous place, but it has been so hideous of late, I hardly know what to think. How can I stay now that Lilian has lost everything and the fates have given me such blessings?'

'Lilian will not blame you for it,' Mary said, clasping Adele's hand. 'I am sure of it. Come on.'

Later, once Reverend Barrett and Anna had left the house to walk Adele home and Lilian excused herself to her bedroom for a rest, Mary sat alone with her thoughts and her notebook. She tapped the pencil against her lip, trying to remember the exact words Adele had said. Did she call Doddingley a dangerous place or an evil one? Where had she heard those phrases before? Mary frowned, annoyed with herself, why couldn't she remember? Though she tried to keep her mind sharp, pregnancy had smoothed its edges. Was there something in the letters? She slid Lilian's letters from their hiding place at the back of the book, scouring the words.

'There,' she said, underlining the descriptions of Doddingley and its community in scratchy pencil strokes.

Mary put the letters down. Why had Adele denied that she was the true author of the letters when she had even used the same phrases? Now she'd heard the same words from Adele's mouth, she was convinced of her penmanship. Thinking back on it, there was something in her manner that was unusual; her response to Donald's entrance into the room had seemed forced, uncomfortable. Had there been a flash of something pass over her face? Irritation? Anger? Was Adele angry that Donald had survived? Mary dropped the pencil and gasped. Was it possible that *Adele* had sought to poison both Donald and Reginald?

CHAPTER SEVENTEEN

'I ought to be very cross with you.' Percy furrowed his brow. 'Running off like that without telling me.'

Mary smothered his face with kisses, which he tried half-heartedly to bat away before swooping her up in his arms then grunting and releasing her down again. He rubbed at his back and nodded towards her pregnant stomach.

'I could still lift you up before you left.'

'Then perhaps my absence has weakened you.' She smiled. 'I can see that I will have to give you more practice.'

'It seems a great many things have changed during my brief absence' Percy replied. All traces of his former sternness had gone, replaced by the delightful softness she knew and loved so well.

'It has only been weeks, but it has felt like years.' Mary pulled him close, enjoying the warmth of his arms around her.

'And you and Claire, friends again?' His eyes twinkled. 'I am very pleased about that.'

'She is much changed. Being a working woman suits her.'

'I think it has more to do with her proximity to a certain infamous poet.'

Mary linked her arm through Percy's, and they walked companionably through the village, stopping to sit on a bench outside the graveyard. The sky above them was marble white, camouflaging the clouds. How quickly the seasons changed and how easily one was replaced by another like a sleight of hand or a card trick. They had to be home for winter, the prospect of being snowed in at Doddingley made her shiver with dread.

'Cold, my love?' Percy put his arm around her. Mary slid into it, not taking her eyes from the sky.

'Not really,' she replied. 'I was just thinking about this place and everything that's happened here. Claire told you about Reginald?'

'Yes, that's a strange affair. What do you think is going on?'

'Well,' Mary whirled round to face him, instantly forgetting the cold. 'I have revised my former theory.'

'I should think so too, now that your original culprit is dead.'

'Oh, I still think Reginald was responsible for more than we know...'

Percy sighed. 'Go on.'

'I don't think he was the intended victim this time,' Mary said, her eyes flashing. 'I think it was a cover to get the actual target.'

On the way back to Lilian's house, Percy had numerous questions. How did the killer know who would take communion first? What if the two men had been feeling chivalrous and had allowed their wives to have taken communion before them? Surely Reginald was always the intended victim?

Mary sighed. She was tiring of Percy trying to find different reasons her theory was wrong and said so.

'I do not say it to be tiresome, Mary, I just worry you are getting too preoccupied with this case. It cannot do either yourself or the baby any good.'

'You cannot think I would put our baby at harm?' she replied, shocked at the very notion. 'And what about Lilian? Her baby will now be brought into this world without a father. What of justice for them? Do they not deserve to know the truth, Percy?'

'Of course they do, but…' Percy shrugged his shoulders. 'I would leave the community to solve their own murders.'

'If you feel that way, then why have you come up here?'

'To bring you home, Mary, to bring you home.'

Later, at the dinner table, all talk of returning home had been taken off the table, and Percy behaved with exquisite politeness to Lilian and her family. Mary simmered with anger. How dare Percy turn up and expect to bring her home like she were a parcel or something that could be returned? This was exactly why she hadn't told him of the trip in the first place. There was no way she would entertain leaving Doddingley until every aspect of the crime had been resolved to her satisfaction. If that riled Percy, so be it.

'Is it thrilling to have Mr Shelley back?' Anna asked, breaking into a wide smile and staring at Percy as if he were a statue of a Greek god come to life.

'Thrilling,' Mary replied, glancing at Percy, who was at that moment trying to fight the temptation to pull apart a bread roll and roll it into his soup. She sighed. Life with a poet was always so glamorous.

'Are you a detective too, Mr Shelley?'

'No, I leave the detecting to Mary. I prefer philosophy and poetry.'

Mary's mind wandered as the rest of the table were treated to a summary of Percy's philosophical ideas and opinion on poetry. It ended, as these things so often did, with a recital of Wordsworth and a speech from *Hamlet*. Usually, Mary enjoyed these performances as much as the other dinner guests, but knowing his desperation to leave Doddingley before the case was concluded had left her in a poor humour.

Mary used the time to consider everything she knew of the case — which admittedly was still far less than she would like to know. Lilian hadn't mentioned the letters, Adele had denied writing them, and there was definitely a chill in the atmosphere between Adele and Donald that hadn't been there on their wedding day. What had caused that? Could it just be that the romance of the proposal and wedding had segued into something more familiar and infinitely less romantic? Surely it was too soon for that, they had only been married a matter of months.

Something else struck her as unusual. Lilian was pregnant, Mary herself was pregnant again, but there was no sign of a child for Donald and Adele. If they had undertaken all the ceremonies of matrimony, then surely progeny was to be expected — but Adele's manner to Donald had been abrasive, harsh, as if she were irritated by his recuperation and recovery. All this pointed to *Adele* being the poisoner, but surely, if she wanted to ensure that Donald was killed, would it not have been easier to find a way of bringing the poison into the household? Cast the finger of suspicion onto someone else.

'I feel like some air,' Mary said, rising from her seat with a swiftness that attracted a table of confused faces.

'Oh, we were retreating to the drawing room. Percy was going to read us some more poems,' Anna replied, her shoulders sinking.

'Another time,' Percy responded. 'I'll come with you, Mary.'

'May I join you?' Anna's enthusiastic voice was a distant bell ringing behind her. Mary walked down the hallway, stopping to pick up her coat. She could hear Percy's consolidatory attempts to placate Anna with yet more promises of this elusive *another time*, which Mary knew would never come if Percy had his way.

Why, he might have ordered the carriage already for all that Mary knew.

No longer caring if she was being polite or rude, Mary opened the door. It was strange to see such an orange sunset after a day of waxy clouds. The sun looked as though it was tearing through the darkness, devouring the tops of trees. She was slower to notice the smell of burning wood, perfuming the air in front of her.

'Percy…' Mary turned back to the house, where Percy was adjusting his dress coat.

'What is it?'

'I think there's a fire?'

Percy swept past her. 'It's coming from the church!'

'Not the church, the rectory,' Lilian cried, pulling her shawl around her shoulders, the rest of the party joining Percy and Mary outside the house, staring down at the village in astonishment as the flames reached into the air. Reverend Barrett stared at her.

'You cannot possibly think of going down there in your condition.'

'We cannot sit here while the village burns,' Lilian replied, pushing his arm away. 'Hurry!'

They ran down the hill towards the village. The villagers rushing around slopping pails of water were lit up by the amber glow of the growing flames, which matched the rising volume of their panic-tinged voices as frantic instructions were thrown around like the water. The entire village was there, every adult hurrying themselves into helpfulness, their children and unruly dogs dancing around in circles, offering no help at all. Fire had torn through the rectory, leaving only its bare bones. Percy and Reverend Barrett grabbed buckets of water, following the directions of Donald, who was conducting the efforts like an orchestra.

'We need more water here!' he yelled, pointing towards a tree. 'If that catches fire, it will take the church with it.' Donald brought a handkerchief up to his face, which was flushed with the heat of the flames. Mary looked around.

'Where's Adele?' she asked Lilian. 'Can you see Adele?'

Lilian shook her head. 'No.'

Mary scanned the faces in the crowd, their features blurring into mirrored expressions of horror and fear, all eyes beset with the same sense of panic. She could not spot Adele among them. But there was Donald, his arms outstretched, yelling instructions so vehemently that the veins pulsed in his neck. Did he presume his wife was amongst these people, trying to save the village?

A loud creak like that of a falling tree sent the villagers darting back as the left side of the rectory abandoned the sky, toppling to the ground. They scurried to it, throwing water with renewed vigour, bucket after bucket drenching the fallen soldier until it finally relinquished its fire and the flames were out.

Cheers accompanied the thick black smoke that rose from the rubble. Mary stepped back and watched as the villagers hugged one another, soot-stained faces returned to former contentment, their previous identities restored. Percy and Reverend Barrett were swept along with it, dancing a merry jig with a couple of women still clutching their buckets in a victory celebration.

In the distance, a solitary shadow in ragged clothing and with scorched hair walked through the rubble, hardly seeming to notice the ash or the smoke. Without the flames licking the night sky, the space had been plunged into darkness, and Mary squinted to see who it was.

'Adele!' Mary tore to her, amazed that the villagers seemed not to have noticed the figure emerging from the depths of the destruction. Was she a ghost?

Mary put an arm around her shaking shoulders. The fabric of her dress flapped in the wind like a ship's sail, bringing the harsh smell of soot and ash to Mary's nostrils. Adele looked at Mary, her features all but obscured by soot, which made her eyes shine.

'I need to speak to you alone,' Adele whispered.

Donald appeared, staring at Adele with his mouth open. Mary expected him to move, but he didn't. He put out his arms, but Adele shrunk back behind Mary.

'Let us walk up the hill,' Adele hissed to her, her voice scratchy under strained breaths.

'As you wish,' Mary replied, linking Adele's arm. 'I will just tell Percy where we are going.'

'No!' Adele cried, shaking her head. 'You mustn't tell Percy; you mustn't tell anyone.'

CHAPTER EIGHTEEN

The smoke from the fire danced in the night sky like a shadow. Mary and Adele climbed up the hill, Adele continuously looking back. Mary sensed a restlessness in her friend; this secrecy was not like her. She'd never seen her so agitated and frightened.

'Here.' Adele pointed to a shed. 'We will talk in here.'

'The gardener's shed?'

'Yes.' Adele opened the door and they slid inside. Mary fumbled in the darkness to avoid the advances of a rake before turning to Adele.

'What is the matter, Adele? Did you get hurt putting out the fire?'

'I did not put out the fire, Mary. I went into the rectory to retrieve the item the council sought to destroy. Here.'

Adele slid a torn piece of paper from her bodice. '*This* is what they were trying to destroy.'

'They?'

'The parish council ... or rather, the remaining parish council.'

'What is it?'

'Proof. I cannot say any more, Mary. Donald will kill me if I do. Let us hope he thinks it lost in the fire, though how I am going to pass off my condition, I do not know. Did you see the way he looked at me? Such anger. I am going away, Mary. I will leave this evening. I had planned it before the fire, but things are moving faster than I had expected. If I do not leave tonight, I will not leave alive.'

Mary hid the piece of paper in her dress, struggling to make sense of what Adele was saying.

'Adele, I do not understand —' she began.

'There is no time for explanation, Mary,' Adele interrupted. 'Once I am safely away, I will write to your home address, but I must take this chance while Donald is distracted by the fire. By now, they will all have gathered at the village hall to talk about rebuilding it, not knowing that the parish council meant to set the building ablaze.'

'Meant to?'

'I overheard them. They intended to start the fire, but I beat them to it. Go to the village hall and keep Donald there. I will be gone in an hour. Thank you, Mary.'

Adele kissed her on the cheek and was gone before Mary could say any more. The chill air from the open door filled the space Adele had vacated and Mary found herself alone in the darkness.

Walking back to the village, the smoke hovered in the frosty sky and only the faintest, bravest stars shone out against the blackness. Mary mind was full of questions. What is on the parchment Adele had given her? She was itching to take a look but knew it may jeopardise Adele's plans. What had Adele meant when she said "I beat them to it"? Had she made her way into the rectory and started the fire? If so, how had she done it? By knocking over a lantern or using a tinderbox? Questions were piling up, one upon another, like a bonfire.

Mary slipped into the village hall unnoticed. She feared it was only a matter of time before the villagers once more turned their attention in her direction. They had been quick to link the murder of the vicar with the presence of outsiders and hadn't Donald — or was it Reginald? — noted that every time Mary visited Doddingley, there was a murder. Well, there hadn't been a murder this time, but there had been a crime.

'Is all well? Were any hurt?' Mary shouted, keen to get her voice heard among the murmuring.

'Thankfully not. Is Adele with you?' Donald asked, his eyes narrowing upon realising that she was not.

'She has returned home; she was fatigued by her efforts at the fire.'

'Adele's efforts were valiant.' The man next to Donald spoke up. Mary had not asked their names before, nor thought of the significance of Reginald and Donald in being members of the parish council. Now, after Adele's warning and pronouncement, she could think of little else. She had been so preoccupied with the notion of Reginald being the killer that she hadn't entertained the possibility there was more than one.

'Even more valiant considering *you* started the fire.' Mary's voice was firm, but her hands trembled at her side. What on earth was she doing? Jumping straight into the snake pit and poking the adder. She spied Percy sitting next to Lilian and Anna. They locked eyes, and he raised his brows at her in a well-known gesture of exasperation. He should know by now that she had a plan. She did have a plan, didn't she? Now the words had left her mouth, she wasn't so sure, and bit her lip as the chorus of disapproval swelled around her. All faces turned towards her, all voices expressed the same disbelief with tutting mouths and shaking heads.

'*I* started the fire?' Donald scoffed. 'I who took charge of the effort to put it out?' He splayed his hands out in front of him, as if encouraging the crowd to gaze upon Mary's stupidity. Now the murmurs turned to loud hisses. Sensing the mood of the room turning rapidly against her, Mary swallowed fast, her heart thudding.

'Months ago, the vicar was shot outside the church on your wedding day, now the rectory is burnt to the ground. I do not think that is a coincidence, do you?'

'No, I do not. But I also know that you yourself were here for both events *and* for the tragic passing of Reginald, which we now know to be caused by a heart attack and not poison. Perhaps the sight of *you* reminded him of all the earlier horror and the shock killed him. Perhaps, Mary Godwin, you are the murderer.'

Mary frowned. Was it her imagination or did the faces of the villagers seem to close in on her? No, they were all still in place, but something had changed and the air seem to swirl in circular shapes around her…

When she came to, she was cradled in Percy's safe arms, and the village hall was empty.

'What happened?' she asked hazily, putting her hand to her forehead.

'You fainted,' Percy replied. 'And just be glad that you did. I thought they were going to cart you off to prison. What were you playing at?' A heavy tread behind him revealed Donald and the men of the parish council. Donald's expression was thunderous.

'I suppose you think that was funny, embarrassing me like that in front of the entire community?'

'I did not say it to embarrass you, I said it because it is true.'

'I did not set fire to the rectory! What a preposterous thing to say.' Donald huffed, turning to the surrounding men, but their faces were not as full of bluster and confidence as his. In fact, Mary would go so far as to say there was a look of guilt passing between them.

'And what was that about Reginald dying of a heart attack?'

'He did. Doctor Snelling told us earlier.'

'Does Lilian know?'

'She does.'

'Right. Well, if that's everything cleared up, I will go now.' Mary got to her feet, using Percy's arm to steady herself. Donald leant towards her, his face uncomfortably close to hers.

'We have had yet another tragedy in your auspicious presence, so I will say this just once. Leave Doddingley. Now. If I must ask you again, it will not be so pleasant as this.'

'Don't worry, I will leave.' Mary swallowed, praying that she'd stalled for long enough and that Adele was on her way out of Doddingley.

Lady Mawdsley had ignored Claire for days. For the first twenty-four hours after her return, she had brooded with alternate huffs and bouts of silence, contemplating whether or not Claire deserved to keep her job. As it was coming up to Christmas and Lady Mawdsley had plans she could not possibly be expected to fulfil on her own, Claire was given a second chance, but it came with conditions. Persephone was to have twice her usual number of walks — both morning and afternoon — of double their previous length, and Claire was to take no time off until Christmas Day, at which she would be given only one day's holiday.

Now, nearing the end of her first week back, Persephone was back to barking enthusiastically at walking times and Lady Mawdsley was back to itching to fill Claire in with all the scandal she'd missed during her trip. After breakfast, Claire was called to the morning room to help Lady Mawdsley plan a festive evening; the old lady deplored London winters, calling them the death of the social season. In most years, she would have gone abroad to Italy or Spain, but the activities on Piccadilly Terrace were keeping her in place.

'You missed all the spectacle of Lady Byron's confinement.'

'Surely there is no excitement in the confinement, only at the end of it.'

'You would not say that if you had seen Lady Byron running around the terrace — not the way for a woman of breeding to behave.' Lady Mawdsley shivered before clamming up, the rest of the information had to be charmed out of her, like a snake.

'I am sure she is content in her confinement, surely the purpose of matrimony is the bringing forth of children. Ow!' Claire sucked her finger where a tiny dot of blood erupted. Even the needlework was resentful of her absence. She had been working on the same bouquet of violets for the duration of her employment with Lady Mawdsley.

'Contentment is not the word I would use for the scene between Lady Byron and Augusta, they were scrapping like dogs.'

Lady Mawdsley grimaced at the memory of it, like she was sucking on an especially bitter lemon.

'Really?' Claire replied, coughing to cover the interest in her voice. 'What were they arguing about?' She turned back to the needlework, determined to feign the nonchalance necessary for Lady Mawdsley's continuation of the topic.

'Lady Byron was accusing Augusta and her brother of —' Lady Mawdsley paused and looked around, as if they were talking indelicately in a society ball, not in her own morning room — 'unnatural acts.'

'Unnatural?'

'Don't be a child, you know what I am referring to.' Lady Mawdsley sighed. 'Needless to say, Augusta is no longer living with the couple.'

Claire's mind struggled to take in everything Lady Mawdsley had just said. If the impropriety she hinted at was the impropriety Claire imagined, surely it would create more of a scandal than being brushed under an expensive carpet and forgotten about? What was it about polite society that delighted in deprivation but shied away from the detail, as if they themselves could get infected by it?

'And you?' Lady Mawdsley peered at Claire like an inquisitive owl. 'Perhaps now you will tell me more of the *emergency* you abandoned me to fix.'

Claire told her about the events at Doddingley, summarising them as concisely as she could, ensuring no detail was left out. Lady Mawdsley listened intently, offering no interruptions except for the occasional pursing of lips and nodding of head. When Claire completed the story, they sat in silence, the only sound between them the mechanical strains of Lady Mawdsley working her jaw — a sure sign that she was thinking deeply about everything Claire had said.

'You say the two men who were poisoned were of the parish council?' she asked.

'Yes.'

'Did you not consider that often it is those with the most power who wield it *unwisely*?' Lady Mawdsley stretched out the last word as if strangling it. 'Reginald and Donald were originally from this village, yes? But Reginald moved away to Scotland and made his fortune in property and business, yes?'

Claire nodded.

'And then returned to Doddingley to repeat the scheme, buying cheap and making money, yes?'

'Yes, but I do not follow…'

'It is clear to me that the men of the council had something to hide and that Reginald — presuming him to be head of the council — was about to blow the whistle on it. Find out what that was, and you will find your murderer.'

Lady Mawdsley sat back, a slow, satisfied smile creeping across her face. She closed her eyes and waved her hand at Claire to leave. It was time for her nap now and doubtless it would be full of scandal and the devilish deeds of others. When she was quiet like this, she possessed a stoic serenity that almost tipped the scales to beauty.

'Don't just stand there staring at me.' Lady Mawdsley opened an eye. 'Go and walk Persephone.'

CHAPTER NINETEEN

'It's just a page torn from a ledger.' Percy shrugged, thrusting the parchment back at Mary. 'I do not see what this proves, Mary.'

'No,' she slumped down on the bed. 'Neither do I. And the one person who could shed light on it has disappeared.'

'Adele?'

She nodded. 'Adele.'

Donald had explained Adele's absence by telling everyone who would listen that she had gone to stay with a friend. It was only a matter of time until he chased after her. But there was clearly something urgent he had to attend to here in Doddingley first, some loose end to be tie up before he could leave. But what was it?

'We know Adele overheard the members of the council planning to set fire to the rectory, presumably for the evidence you have here.' Percy pointed at the parchment Adele had given Mary. 'We also know that someone wanted Reginald silenced, perhaps relying on his being more advanced in years to make the dose of poison deadly to him, but not to others.'

'I would presume that Reginald insisted on taking communion first,' Mary added. 'He wasn't the sort of man to be chivalrous in such matters. So perhaps the killer knew that, depended on that? And if that was the case, there would be little risk of harm to the other members of the council, not if Reginald had taken the lion's share of the poison.' Mary gathered her thoughts. 'And Adele would not let me talk to Donald while he was recuperating. I took that to be wifely concern, but now I think she was concerned only with her own plans.'

'Do you still believe the letters to have been written by her?'

'Yes.' Mary nodded. 'By drawing my attention to Lilian and her plight, it distracted me from Adele and hers.'

'Perhaps now a date has been set for the funeral, you may speak to Lilian about Reginald.'

'I think you are right.' Mary sighed. 'I know that the timing is not ideal, but time is running out. If we don't solve this case before Donald concludes whatever is keeping him here, Adele's murder will be next.'

When they arrived at the Big House, Anna was playing the piano, her upright posture a sharp contrast with the jumble of fingers upon keys, a vague approximation of a waltz.

'It is no use.' Anna dragged herself slowly from the piano stool. 'I will never be able to play properly.'

'You are coming along handsomely,' Reverend Barrett soothed. 'You just need to keep practising.'

The spacious drawing room was dressed in a gentle green, the colour of sage, two gilt mirrors on opposite walls reflecting the Reverend Barrett and his daughters back into the room. Lilian's stomach looked like it had been placed on her lap, a precious, heavy weight for her to carry. She wore a pale white gown which emphasised her pale face and sleep-deprived eyes. Was it the advanced pregnancy, or not having an answer to Reginald's death that kept her awake at night?

'We shall have tea!' Anna brightened and left the room.

Now they were alone with Lilian and her father, Mary extracted the torn ledger page from her bag and passed it to Reverend Barrett.

'Do you have any idea what this is?'

The old man peered closely, taking out his monocle to scrutinise the parchment.

'Parish tithes by the look of it, and a lot tidier than mine. I do miss Reginald helping with parish matters.' Reverend Barrett squeezed the monocle from his eye and sighed.

Mary thought back to the reverend's cluttered office, the carpet of paperwork. He was clearly out of his depth without Reginald's support.

'What are tithes?'

'Earnings. Paid to the parish.'

'Would the council have to pay the parish?'

'They would collect it all and be responsible for their own and for men of wealth and power like Donald and Reginald, it would be a sizeable amount.'

Mary took the paper, running her eyes up and down the list of names and sums. It was true, all the villagers were there with ticks by most of the names. Only a handful of names had the word "outstanding" beside them.

'Look at this.' Percy handed her another sheet of paper.
'It's a list of the members of the Farmer's Council.' Mary took the list, compared it to the list of outstanding debts. It matched. 'It says that the tithes were payable in April?'

'Yes, that would be standard. Some pay monthly, others by season, depending on their trade.'

'But for men such as Donald...' Mary trailed off. She thought it better to keep Reginald's name out of it, for now.

'Then it looks like they would have paid their accounts in April.'

Mary turned to Lilian. 'Did you not say you were surprised by the speed of Donald's courtship of Adele? That his interest seemed to pique after her father died?'

'Well, yes,' Lilian replied. 'I am unsure where you are going with this.'

'Presumably the death of Reverend Clarke would slow down the processes of obtaining outstanding debts?' Mary shrugged, looking over at Percy, who knew far more about being in debt than she did.

'I would say it would,' he agreed. 'And if a new vicar came to a small village like this, I would think it is easier to hide outstanding arrears.'

'Particularly if his record keeping is as lapse as mine,' Reverend Barrett said, with a wry chuckle.

'Lilian, I have to ask you this, though it pains me to do it, was Reginald troubled by anything? Did you notice anything different about him in the months after the wedding?'

Lilian shook her head. 'He seemed distracted and busy, but then he always was.' She hesitated. 'He was aggravated by your coming to the wedding and quite angry with Adele for inviting you. He passed it off as morality, but I sensed there was more to it than that. It was almost as if your coming here had ruined some plan.'

Mary froze. Of course! She saw it all now.

'We need to get you all out of Doddingley and back to Dundee as quickly as possible, there is no time to waste.'

'But it is Reginald's funeral tomorrow — I cannot leave now!' Lilian wiped a tear from her eye. Her father shook his head.

'No, Mary, it is quite impossible. We cannot leave until we have paid our respects. It is already agreed that Lilian will come back to Dundee with us once the funeral is completed, but not before.'

'Then we must pray we are not too late.'

*

Mary had always held the notion that winter was the best time for funerals, just as springtime was the best for weddings. Anything out of this natural order seemed … unnatural. There was something about the harshness of the naked landscape, the stripped-back sparsity of it that welcomed death. The funeral cortège moved slowly across the frosty path, the delicate winter flowers and grasses bowing their heads in solemnity as Lilian followed the coffin into the church. Her mourning attire was a perfect bloom of stiff serenity, and the church bells punctuated her steps, peeling through the building in booming echoes of grief. Mary gripped her bag tightly as Donald passed by, taking his place in the pew in front of theirs.

The church swelled with the entire village. Mary scrutinised the faces of the mourners, all looked suitably solemn. Even those wronged by Reginald, like Mrs Harris, concealed their true feelings. Mary's heart raced like a pocket watch, counting down the minutes until they could leave Doddingley, find Adele, and restore Lilian to the safety of Dundee.

A sermon was given, a summing-up of Reginald's life. Mary was surprised to learn that he was only forty-nine. He had always seemed much older. Still, he'd had eleven more years of life than her mother did. She dare not allow her mind to do the calculations for Clara.

Eventually the service came to an end and the body of Reginald was laid to rest on the hilly incline at the back of the graveyard, near to the Reverend Clarke's resting place. If Reginald was responsible for the vicar's murder, then he would have opportunity enough to atone from the next world. The sound of horses' hooves made Mary turn. She nodded at Percy, who made a discreet path away from the mourners, darting back down the hill in the direction of the carriage. Donald took out his pocket watch, looking at it as Lilian delivered a stem of rosemary on the top of the coffin.

Mary kept her eyes on Donald, whose face seemed oddly pink in the cool air. He continually looked about him, stopping now and then to wipe a bead of sweat from his forehead. Final prayers were said, and the altar boy, Charles, lead the cross and the mourners back to the church. When they arrived at the turning where the carriage had been, it was no longer there and Mary watched Donald's head swivel in panic, looking this way and that way.

'Are you looking for something?' Mary asked.

'Mind your own business,' Donald hissed through clenched teeth as the mourners dispersed back to their homes. Once they were alone, Donald seized Mary's hand.

'Where is it? What have you done with it?'

'You're going to have to be more specific,' Mary replied. 'Are you talking about the document outlining your unpaid tithes, or the carriage you hired to find and kill Adele?'

'What are you talking about?' He let go of her hand, which throbbed painfully. 'I want to find Adele, not kill her. You have murder on the brain. You might want to go and see a doctor about that. Take after your mother.'

Anger rushed through her. 'Men like you see any woman with a mind of her own as dangerous. How quickly did you realise Adele would not take on the part of a meek wife —?'

Mary's words were cut off by a thick hand at her throat. 'If you know where Adele is, you had better tell me or I will kill you both.' She struggled under his grasp. Her hands found purchase on his, scratching at his iron grip until she broke the skin; the momentary release that followed was enough to enable her to bite his hand and raise her leg high enough to knee him between the legs. Donald recoiled, and Mary ran.

'Fire! Fire!' she shouted as she ran. Soon, she was close enough to the mourners for them to turn around. 'Grab Donald!' she pleaded. Reverend Barrett and a few of the village men did as Mary asked. Donald twisted under their grip.

'Get everyone to the village hall,' Mary said, before collapsing onto the ground. Anna rushed to help her.

'Are you hurt?'

'Quite the reverse: the last piece of the puzzle has finally slotted into place.'

CHAPTER TWENTY

'Did you tell the driver where to wait?' Mary asked Percy, who had just arrived, breathless, at the village hall.

Percy smiled. 'I did. It has cost me — my pockets are almost empty — but he will take us to Dundee and then home again.'

Mary looked over at Donald, who was snarling like a caged animal under the restraint of Reverend Barrett and the men of the village. The rest of the mourners watched on with interest.

'What is the meaning of this?' he shouted. 'On what authority do you bring me here?'

'I have no authority other than the quest for justice and the truth. These villagers have every right to know who is behind the murders that have *poisoned* their village.'

'They already do! We know the chimney sweep Timothy Lakin killed Reverend Clarke, then killed himself because of the guilt.' Donald burst free and circled the villagers. 'Why are you listening to someone whose arrival here has brought nothing but death? Haven't we been plagued with a six-month melancholy that started when she —' he thrust a shaking finger in Mary's direction — 'came to Doddingley, bringing all her poison with her? Why are you good people listening to a heathen? See how she bewitched a married man with her siren call? Her words are as venomous as the poison she put in the communion cup.'

There was a collective gasp from the villagers and all faces turned towards her. Mary's blood boiled in her veins, igniting the furnace of anger that was fuelled by injustice. If Donald wanted a fight, then he'd have one. It was laughable, really, his desperate attempts to throw the shadow of suspicion on her;

even calling her a siren. She would remember that, and demand Percy write an ode with her as a siren at its centre, but not until the people of Doddingley had answers.

'Donald Pinder always fancied himself as a squire, but he lacked the business acumen of his ancestors and soon gambled away the property he had inherited, leaving it open for his old friend Reginald to buy up.' Mary found her voice as she walked amongst the villagers. 'When Reginald joined the parish council, he discovered Donald's habit of not paying his tithes and, having been responsible for the upkeep of his father-in-law's accounts, he knew exactly how to hide it. Donald's sudden wooing of Adele following the death of her father was an opportunity to claw back the money and status he felt he had lost, and the marriage would give him respectability.'

Mary paused. If only Adele were here to back her up. She had learnt the secret of Donald's deception, but when? Adele had been too fearful for her own life to stay. Mary continued. 'When Reverend Clarke announced that the wedding would be his last public duty before his retirement, Donald spotted his chance. Donald and Reginald paid Timothy Lakin to kill Reverend Clarke and leave the village, but when Lakin came back and tried to blackmail Donald, he strangled him and made it look as though he'd taken his own life. This was the scene Reginald and Percy found.'

'Monstrous! Preposterous!' Donald huffed, surveying Mary through narrowed eyes. 'You do not have a shred of proof for any of your claims. It is nothing but fantasy.'

'You're right, I didn't, but you hadn't reasoned on Reginald's conscience. With a baby on the way, he was haunted by what he had done and came close to telling Lilian on several occasions.'

'That's right,' Lilian gasped. 'He seemed distracted lately. He did not seem so eager to attend the council meetings or visit Donald, they used to be so close. I should have known it meant something.'

Lilian winced, put her hand to her stomach.

'Are you well?'

'It will pass. It always does.' Lilian breathed heavily and stroked her stomach.

'Please conclude this winter's tale of yours. I would like to cleanse myself of the dirt you are throwing at me,' Donald snickered. The rest of the hall laughed with him. Mary's spirits sank, but Percy nodded encouragement at her, and the expectant faces of Lilian, Reverend Barrett and Anna confirmed she had to carry on — she could not stop now.

'You knew Reginald was feeling guilty, and you feared it was only a matter of time until he revealed your secret so you poisoned the chalice. You yourself only sipped at it, but Reginald was a religious man who took the sacrament seriously and drank it devoutly.'

'*You* killed Reginald?' Lilian stammered, all colour draining from her face as she collapsed into her father's arms. Anna leapt forward, ready to scratch or hit Donald, but Percy jumped in, holding her back.

'He is not worth your anger,' he soothed, holding Anna back.

'I suppose you are going to accuse me of the fire at the rectory now?' Donald spat. 'Make for the full set?'

'No, on that charge you are innocent, but only because someone beat you to it.'

'And why, out of curiosity, would I want to set fire to the rectory?'

'Because the new vicar was going through the tithes and was sure to discover your unpaid bills.'

'If that were true, would it not be easier to steal the records rather than raise a fire?' Donald sniggered. 'It seems a little extreme.'

'A fire may have many causes, stealing one item draws attention to its importance.'

A scream suddenly ripped through the air. It came from Lilian who was collapsed on the floor, her teeth bared in agony.

'She's having the baby!' Anna cried. 'Quickly!'

Mary and Percy rushed to Lilian's side. The villagers seemed to forget the object of their previous inquiry and all turned to Lilian, coming together to help transport her from the village hall back to the Big House. This was the community at its best, coming together for some good news, a shining star of hope amongst all the sorrow. Mary looked back, curious to locate Donald among the crowd, but saw him running away, back past the village hall and off in the opposite direction.

EPILOGUE

'You are sure I look presentable?' Claire fussed at her dress, pulling up the neckline and smoothing down the arms before walking over to the mirror and performing the same action with her hair. Mary stood behind her, clasping her sister by the shoulders.

'You look perfect, Claire. You have blossomed into quite the English rose.'

'Do I detect a hint of jealousy in your tone, Mary?'

'No, not at all.' Mary rubbed at her spine; her swollen stomach and ankles made her feel anything but blooming. Blooming uncomfortable but glad to be back in Windsor.

It would soon be time for her confinement. Lilian had given birth to a son, Charles, weeks earlier; sharing the good news with Mary and Percy via letter. She had returned to Dundee to live with her family, hoping that the new year would bring a new start. Once their own child was safely delivered, Mary and Percy would go to Dundee to see them, introduce their children and hope that the bonds of friendship would stretch across the miles. She could not wait to reacquaint herself with Dundee and Edinburgh, to walk up the dark steps and dream of monsters and gothic passageways. Her stomach tightened. Talking of monsters, there was still no news of Donald, or of Adele, to her infinite regret. Wherever she was, Mary hoped she was happy and safe.

'Tell me, Claire, are you nervous at the prospect of seeing Lord Byron again?'

'Yes,' Claire sighed. Mary had stopped asking about Claire's correspondence with Lord Byron upon their return from

Doddingley. Claire's sly smiles and shy giggles whenever his name was mentioned confirmed their continued correspondence and that there was more between them than was proper. Lady Byron's patience with her erstwhile husband had finally snapped not two weeks into the new year — the snow had thawed more quickly than she had — and it was clear to Mary that Claire had willingly taken up the slack of whatever aspect of their relationship Byron missed. Claire had begged Mary for a meeting between her, Percy and Byron, and, confined to the house in Windsor and with Percy away on another London errand until the weekend, Mary had finally agreed to a high tea.

Whatever she had been expecting from Byron, it wasn't this, and as he held out a hand to her, Mary could not help but notice his pronounced limp, the shake of his outstretched hand, and the dark expression that swept over his face like a black cloud. She who had been spoilt by Percy's angelic sweetness, thought he had far more in common with the monster of her nightmares; it was as much as Mary could do to stop herself from inhaling sharply at the sight of him and crying out in recognition, "You!"

Byron surveyed her with the same level of inquisition — as if he were trying to trace every aspect of Mary Wollstonecraft's face in hers. Mary blushed under his scrutiny of her face and swollen belly, while she folded her hands to disguise the continued absence of a wedding ring — she only noticed such things when with someone of an elevated social class and however reckless Byron might be in his personal life, there was no denying his eminent social position. Percy would kick himself when he found out he'd missed this opportunity, so the pressure was on for Mary to ensure she made a good enough impression for there to be a renewed acquaintance.

The regal reds, golds and blacks of Byron's outfit made Mary's drawing room seem anaemic in comparison and she felt just as colourless compared to the symmetry of Claire's red and black velvet gown, Claire's hair tied up in the very Parisian style they had mocked two years earlier. It seemed like much longer. They were all so altered. How much would the new year change them? Would 1816 bring the seismic changes of the previous two years? Mary felt like she had aged a decade in this time, though the calendar reminded her she was still — in society's eyes — young and impressionable.

'Thank you for agreeing to meet with me,' Byron said, slipping into a reclining pose completely impractical for the drinking of tea. 'I am a great admirer of your mother's work, your father's too…'

Mary flushed at the reminder of her parents, both of whom may well have been dead. They had spent a second Christmas shunned by her family, but she would have her own child this year and this time nothing would go wrong.

The afternoon passed pleasantly, Mary and Byron conversed easily on subjects of philosophy and poetry and when he left, he gave her a copy of his latest book. Claire watched them as if it were sport or a fascinating play she could not take her eyes off, her gaze alternately landing on Mary, as if willing her to be erudite and charming, or to Byron, where it could not disguise the depth of affection that ran like a river beneath it. Byron made his excuses, shook Mary's hand, and kissed Claire's. Something in his manner made her genuinely afraid of the impact he would have on Claire's life. She could not help but fear that Byron's influence would shape her life long after the memory of his kisses had faded.

Once he was safely back in his carriage and on his way home, Claire collapsed on the settle as if in a swoon.

'Oh, Mary, is he not the most sublime creature in the world?'

'He is certainly charming and *very* confident.'

'But wouldn't you be as confident if you had all his gifts?' Claire sat up, replaced the swooning gesture with a frantic flapping of her hands as if cooling her face with a fan. 'I can scarcely keep control of my senses when I am around him.'

'Yes, I can see that.'

'He liked you too, I can see the two of you will become great friends.'

'Alas, the friendship will be all too brief, as Percy has plans for us to go abroad once the baby is born.' The baby kicked, no longer the faint fluttering of a butterfly, now it felt like a punch. He was certainly a strong and determined baby.

'I was thinking of that,' said Claire. 'Lady Mawdsley tells me that Geneva is a wonderful place for a writer, she is thinking of taking a house there in the summer.'

'Geneva? And will you be accompanying her?'

'No, Lady Mawdsley prefers to travel alone. But I have saved some money from working for her and I had thought that perhaps I might travel. It is time I gave some real thought to my true vocation in life.'

'Have you given up your dream of being the wife of a great poet?' Mary mocked. She had long since given up dreams of becoming Percy's wife; with another child on the way, it no longer seemed such an important bond.

'I do not think I have it in me to become a wife,' Claire said, smiling. 'I think history will remember me as one of Byron's muses. But I have no intention of chasing around the world after him alone.'

'Chasing after him? Am I to presume that Byron is planning a trip to Geneva?' Mary sighed.

'He may have mentioned such a scheme...' Claire shrugged.

Mary took a deep breath. She knew when Claire had a plan, and she also knew that she could not be trusted to go on her own, heaven only knew what disasters might befall her. Switzerland had seemed charming from their brief trip through it on their Petite Tour.

'Well then, may 1816 be a year of travel and adventure,' Mary said.

Claire smiled. 'To travel and adventure!'

'Just promise me one thing?' Mary shook her head. 'No more murders!'

A NOTE TO THE READER

Dear Reader,

Following her elopement with Percy Shelley in the summer of 1814, Mary Godwin Wollstonecraft's life upon their return to London lacked the same sparkle and excitement. Instantly plunged into debt, living from hand to mouth, Mary soon found herself pregnant and Percy largely absent, as he alternated between dodging creditors and trying to find new sources of revenue. This pattern of behaviour dominated much of the autumn and winter months of 1814, and this dark time is reflected in the more sombre themes of *The Lost Girls*.

By summer 1815, things had got worse. Their baby daughter Clara was born prematurely in February 1815 and died twelve days later, on 6th March 1815. Mary's journal entry on Sunday, 19th March tells us something about her state of mind at the time: "Dreamt that my little baby came to life again — that it had only been cold and that we rubbed it by the fire and it lived — I awake and find no baby — I think about the little thing all day — not in good spirits." The simplicity and naivety of the dream reminds us that Mary was still only seventeen at the time of this tragedy.

In the brief gestation of her relationship with Percy, Mary had encountered much penury and hardship, and it is testimony to her tremendous strength of character that she used all the challenges to learn and become more open-hearted. In this book, I wanted to give Mary the opportunity to connect to happier times and remember a period where she had been on the precipice of adulthood and exploring everything that meant. In 1812 Mary's father, William Godwin, sent her to stay with the Baxter family in Dundee; wealthy textile merchants who owned mills. Though she received no formal education in Scotland, Mary honed her literary imagination there, enjoying evenings spent with Isabel Baxter discussing gothic literature and great romantic heroes and heroines, and exploring the architecture of the Dundee docks and the gothic steps that swirled around The Cottage (the mansion at which Mary stayed). Dundee provided fertile ground for her imagination, and she would utilise its dark streets and wild storms over the Tay to great effect in *Frankenstein*.

In this novel, I have transformed the Baxters into the Barretts, and Mr Baxter from a textile baron into a vicar. Artistic license has allowed me to introduce another friend, Adele Somerton, into the storyline and to create two husbands — Reginald and Donald — that have taken on young brides and moved them away from Dundee. Donald and Adele's wedding allowed Percy and Mary to escape from the heartbreak of Windsor and takes them on a journey where their dependency on each other in a sea of unfriendly locals would remind them of their underlying love. Despite everything, Mary and Percy are soulmates, and the events that take place in this book go some way to healing the rift that had developed between them and threatened, at the start of the book, to engulf them.

I used the timeline of Mary's life to think of a natural path that would take Claire Clairmont out of the picture and bring Lord Byron into it. In 1815, following the death of Clara and the much-contested question of whether (or not) she burnt the nursery furniture and Clara's scant possessions, Claire was sent to Lynmouth on the north Devon coast. She wrote to their sister Fanny on 28th May: "Mary writes to me that you thought me unkind in not letting you know before my departure; indeed I meant no unkindness, but I was afraid if I told you that it might prevent my putting a plan into execution which I preferred before all the Mrs Knapps in the world…"

I substituted Devon for London and have played around a little with the actual timeline of Claire meeting Byron (it actually took place in winter 1815, but is slightly earlier in this book). Claire becomes a companion to a wealthy London lady, Lady Mawdsley, as a means of bringing her into contact with Byron. I had great fun writing about Claire's adventures with Persephone. There is something about Claire's character that made a pampered pooch nemesis a natural fit somehow. Of all the ancillary characters I have written, I have enjoyed writing Madame Thibeaux (in *The Missing Wife*) and Lady Mawdsley the most. When I was a young girl, my mother worked as a carer for older ladies, one of whom was a phenomenal woman called Mrs Drinkwater who was fiercely intelligent, exceptionally ahead of her time and the most stubborn woman I have ever met. Both Madame Thibeaux and Lady Mawdsley have something of her personality weaved into them.

I am delighted that we got to meet Lord Byron in this book. I have a longstanding fascination with him and love his poetry; let's face it, everyone loves a bad boy. Although several of Byron's poems inspired later operas and ballets, I could not find any evidence of this in the timeframe I was using; so again, I have used literary license here. The lives of all the heroes are the framework from which I create the tapestry of events, but the fine detail is not always historically accurate; I hope you will forgive me and have enjoyed the latest journey with Mary, Percy, Claire and now Byron.

If you enjoyed *Death at the Altar* and would feel comfortable leaving a review on **Amazon** or **Goodreads** that would be greatly appreciated. I hope you have enjoyed your adventure with Mary and Percy and will join them on their next adventure! I'm always delighted to hear from my readers, so if you would like to connect with me then please follow me at **@donnagowlandwrites** on Instagram and **@DLGowlandWrites** on X.

Sapere Books is an exciting new publisher of brilliant fiction and popular history.

To find out more about our latest releases and our monthly bargain books visit our website:
saperebooks.com